Portia was born and raised in Melbourne, Victoria, to Estonian parents who migrated to Australia after World War II. She has worked in the retail, telecommunications and real estate sectors. Always wanting to be a writer, over the years, she has edited and written articles and reviews for various university student newspapers and independent publications.

She currently lives with her son in the picturesque Gilbert Valley region, South Australia, nestled between the wine-growing regions of the Barossa and Clare Valleys.

In her spare time, Portia is busy working away on her next book projects, which will include the sequel to her debut novel *The Big Dead Dry*.

For my parents, Eha and Edur, who always believed in me,
and to my real Ricardo.

Portia Stanton-Noble

THE BIG DEAD DRY

Copyright © Portia Stanton-Noble (2021)

The right of Portia Stanton-Noble to be identified as the author of this work has been asserted by the author in accordance with section 77 and 78 of the Copyright, Designs and Patents Act 1988.

All rights reserved. No part of this publication may be reproduced, stored in a retrieval system, or transmitted in any form or by any means, electronic, mechanical, photocopying, recording, or otherwise, without the prior permission of the publishers.

Any person who commits any unauthorised act in relation to this publication may be liable to criminal prosecution and civil claims for damages.

This is a work of fiction. Names, characters, businesses, places, events, locales, and incidents are either the products of the author's imagination or used in a fictitious manner. Any resemblance to actual persons, living or dead, or actual events is purely coincidental.

A CIP catalogue record for this title is available from the British Library.

ISBN 9781528990097 (Paperback)
ISBN 9781528990103 (ePub e-book)

www.austinmacauley.com

First Published (2021)
Austin Macauley Publishers Ltd
25 Canada Square
Canary Wharf
London
E14 5LQ

Writing this work of fiction has been both fun and satisfying for me. But on the serious side, I do have to first acknowledge my grandmother Paula Teppich's influence, who was always engaged and interested in my creative endeavours from childhood. In her own quiet way, she encouraged me to always do my best.

I also have to acknowledge the inspirational local writers I met in 2019 who attended a writers' event in Saddleworth, South Australia. It was an event which I was proud to be personally involved with and it inspired me to finish what I had started.

Chapter One

She drove into the small town of Brumby Flat, welcomed by the long avenue of tall gumtrees, majestic palms and pine trees lining the road verge. Her passenger, using his youthful powers of perception, took in the surroundings and made a mental note about the dry and dusty terrain. Unwittingly, she was driving straight into a small town stricken with drought and teeming with secrets.

Arriving at their destination, they both climbed out of the car. They both looked up and down the quiet main street. There were only a handful of locals walking around. They seemed to agree before even a word was said between them. It was evident to anyone watching that they were related to each other as they reflected the same body language.

Finally, her very tall son spoke, "You know, if we move here, we're living further out. This is the true, true country," he said.

"Yes, I know. But look at what we get. Two houses for the price of one. Like wow," Raquel Willaston replied, swinging her arms around, palms out, "I know your grandmother said no. Too much work here she said, but I am sure that we can do something with the shop part. Don't you think?"

He gave her his trademark lopsided smile and brushed his auburn tinged hair off his face, "I think you've made up your mind. If I can get internet signals here, I'll be happy."

"Oh yeah, did you notice something strange too?" he added suddenly.

Raquel arched an eyebrow, "What, honey?"

"Where are all the men? So many women in town, I am totally outnumbered."

"Really? I haven't noticed. I'm sure it's not like that. The men are probably working around the district. Out of town somewhere. There would be plenty of farmers around."

He rolled his eyes, which were the same hazel colour of hers, "Sure. You're too busy to see these things. Work, work, work. Anyway, we'd better look quick and go. It's getting late. We both have to work soon."

Raquel had lost track of time. She had a final glance at the early twentieth-century five-bedroom house and the attached shop of roughly the same size. Both had nice shady verandas. Inside, some of the floors sloped and there was a touch of salt damp on the outer wall facing the corner. That's all she could find fault with. The bargain price was the best part. Two buildings for the price of one. That meant something to her. Also, the chance to make a fresh new start in a new town appealed to her. In her mind, she was escaping her tumultuous past.

"Okay, I am happy. Let's go. This is our new home. And this is our new town."

Raquel started the car and they were soon on their way back home. As they had over an hour of country driving ahead of them, Raquel had time to think about what she should say to Ricardo. He was a long-time ex-lover who had told her he would catch up with her that day at her workplace. Should she be cool and calm, or conversational and warm towards him? She wasn't exactly sure which way to react. They had not seen each other for three years, two months and five days.

Unfortunately, she was worrying herself for no reason. At that precise moment, Ricardo was still working hard in the Adelaide Central Business District. He had been thinking about Raquel all day. All week in fact, however, he had a pile of paperwork to get through as the firm's trainee accountant. There was also another problem. Since he had moved up into an office job and moved his family into an apartment in the city, he had swapped his old fire engine red nineteen-eighties Torana for a canary yellow 50cc motorcycle. He thought it was a great swap as he could zip around the CBD. He had never considered he would need to chase his former favourite city girl Raquel so far out into the countryside. The 50cc would not make it that far out.

Life has a funny way of twisting and then turning things completely upside down. Ricardo knew this better than most. When Raquel worked in the Adelaide CBD, Ricardo was residing in the outer suburbs and driving a forklift in bright yellow overalls for a living. Then, she scored lucky in an inheritance and ended up having a tree change and meanwhile, Ricardo got the office job he had always wanted, to try to get closer to her. Now distance and circumstance had successfully separated them. It would be hard to reverse their respective good fortunes now.

Ricardo had all the trappings of his new hipster existence. Two tailored suits he can match with his royal blue polka dot tie, his own office, a desk, a leather swivel chair, a laptop and two drawers full of stationary. The trainee accountant gig required a lot of discipline from Ricardo. He had managed to change his language to a pleasant one word of profanity in every spoken sentence. In his forklift truck days, he was rough and tough, and his sentences were short and liberally peppered with profanities. He had come a long way since then. His clients often leaned forward in the chair opposite and only drew back and grimaced at his odd swear word. Then they leaned forward again, hanging expectantly on his good grasp of all their dodgy tax returns.

Now he sat as far back as he could into his leather chair without toppling over. He started to reminisce on how he had met Raquel Willaston over twenty years ago.

They had met over a packet of lifesavers at the local corner shop where Raquel was working on weekends. She was a high school student finishing off her year twelve. As soon as they met, they got on like a house on fire and laughed like old friends over silly trivial things. He charmed her with his Roman nose and obvious Italian dark good looks. She liked his ridiculously short work shorts which further emphasised his well-shaped buttock cheeks. The only drawback was that he stood two inches shorter than her.

After coming into the corner shop a couple of times, he finally got up enough courage to ask her out to dinner. They went out twice to seafood restaurants and both times, she ended up in the restaurant bathroom, being sick after the meals. He had to drive her home, with her head sticking half over the passenger window of his old Torana. It was not the romantic sexy scenario he had been patiently waiting for.

After that, Raquel was too busy studying for her year twelve exams. She had two weeks to cram nine months' worth of six school subjects into her head. It was a frantic final flurry for her. Ricardo backed off into the background and waited for her to make the next move.

She sat the exams and then the final day of high school came around. It was the day when year twelve students went crazy, dressed up and pulled dozens of pranks on their teachers.

Raquel arrived at school that morning, in her very unusual choice of costume. Surrounded by popstar lookalikes, television characters and movie stars, Raquel came to school dressed as her favourite historical character. Marie-Antoinette. She had a white beehive wig perched precariously on her head and a seventeenth-century full dress with bunches of pale petticoat underneath. It was not a sensible choice as it was a summery thirty-two degrees in the shade. Her petite ornamental fan did nothing to stop her powdery white makeup from running into her buxom tanned, well corseted cleavage. Because of her costume, she felt like an outsider. She was not included in the pranks, and anyway, it was hard to run about on a hot day in layers of synthetic fabric. She eventually did the only thing a girl could do – she called Ricardo.

He dropped everything and drove like a sex-crazed maniac, which he was by now, to the gates of her high school. His treasured Torana was in for a service that day, so Ricardo had to borrow his best mate's shiny jet-black Harley. He was outfitted in his usual T-shirt with short shorts and Doc Martens. For road safety, fortunately, he was wearing a helmet.

He roared to a skidding halt in the school main courtyard, with the Harley shimmering in the sunlight. Students 'oooohhhh-ed' and 'aaahhhh-ed' while teachers frowned and snorted their displeasure. Raquel squealed with delight and gathered her petticoats for a run-up to Ricardo and his amazing black machine. She took off her white beehive wig and tossed it into the crowd of students like it was a wedding bouquet.

She bunched up her seventeenth-century dress with care to straddle the bike and planted herself behind Ricardo, wrapping her arms around his waist. Before the teachers had time to react, they roared off and zipped through the front gates, disappearing in a plume of thick, black smoke. The Harley also needed a service. But Ricardo didn't care. This was his big moment to shine as an Italian stallion should.

They drove until rows of neat front yards and houses gave way to avenues of trees and rolling hills. And the petrol ran out. Ricardo pushed the Harley off the country road and propped it up against a tree by a trickling creek. Raquel smiled at him shyly and raised her skirt and petticoats past her knees. She had whispered to him earlier that she never wore panties and she proved it to him then. They made frantic love there on the banks of that creek, under a pale cloudless blue sky. A small group of cows stood in the next paddock watching them between plucking at and chewing grass.

After their lovemaking, they rang for a taxi using Raquel's mobile phone.

The next day, Ricardo told her the truth. He had been seeing her, but he was also seeing his fiancé at the same time. Ricardo explained to her that he was confused but certain he was going to go ahead and marry his fiancé. Raquel cried for days. Then she got on with her life. The problem was Ricardo drifted in and out of it, which made her think they could have a future together one day.

Present-day was no different. As Raquel arrived at her work, she called Ricardo on her mobile.

"Hey, where are you?" she asked.

"I am fuckin' sorry, babe. Still in the city. Have a shit load of paperwork to do."

Raquel sighed audibly, "You're standing me up again?"

He toppled forward into his chair, "No, not really. Fuck. I want to see you but you have to understand, I am far away, and I have a fuckin' small bike. It's not going to make it up to where you are, shit, there's just no way."

This was the last straw for Raquel, "Okay Rick, I give up. On your bike. I am not going to sit around all day today waiting for you…or anyone else to turn up."

"Wait, wait," he cried, "I want to see you, I miss you, babe. Do you think I am making up excuses?"

"Goodbye Rick."

She had hung up. He shrugged his shoulders and resolved to wait for her to call him back one day. He might have a new plan by then. He went back to playing Tetris and Solitaire on his mobile phone.

In the meantime, Raquel logged onto her laptop and started tapping away on the keys furiously.

"I am going home early today." She snarled at her boss as he strolled cautiously past her office. He was terrified of her. She was a good solid worker when she was in the office, but he found her moods difficult to fathom.

"But you just got in…" his voice trailed off. He was too afraid to finish the sentence.

"Flexiday." She replied sharply.

"Oh yes," he nodded and hastily disappeared out of sight.

She got the information she needed and stormed out. Ricardo had let her down again but she was determined to enjoy her night. She had made a date online with a man she had been emailing through a dating app. He had responded and said to meet him at a well-known city pub. She had a long two-hour drive ahead of her but it was worth it for the romantic dinner he promised and to hear a few nice compliments.

As she drove to her romantic rendezvous, her date was preparing to meet her. He was a secretive type. In fact, he was not going to present her with his real persona. On the dating app, he gave his name as Jason the security guard when he was actually Senior Detective Phillip Duncan. He always had a problem with the ladies when he said he was a detective, so he changed his story to suit. He was not particularly handsome, but he was at least tall, had some hair, shaved very short and his eyes were a bright sky blue behind his glasses. His unusual childhood upbringing had a lot to do with his mannerisms and secretive nature.

Senior Detective Phillip Duncan was born to a couple of hippies from the nineteen-seventies. They were travelling around Australia, enjoying popular and obscure music festivals in their kombi van when his mother realised, she had a baby on the way. Phillip Duncan who had been unofficially 'christened' Byron Sunbury Campbell to begin with, arrived into the world on the sand dunes of Byron Bay, New South Wales. His mother was sunbathing topless and lightly strumming a guitar when she started feeling waves of contractions.

They were kind parents, if a little bit absent-minded. But the nineteen-seventies were all about sex, being free and experimenting with substances. Sometimes they accidentally left their son behind at a remote service station, but they remembered sometime after and would return to pick him up. The first four formative years of his young life, his home was the kombi van, or a tent hastily pitched up by the side of a country road. He learnt to sleep through days and nights of music festivals.

He was also one of the rare children who ate his vegetables as it was the primary food of choice of his strictly vegan parents.

As he outgrew his clothes so quickly, they dressed him eventually in knitted ponchos which were trendy wear at the time, and pyjama pants which were not.

Because of their nomadic and gypsy-like existence, little Byron was not allowed to keep a pet on the road. He would bring stray cats, dogs and any wild bird with a broken wing home to the kombi van, but his parents would firmly say no. He did catch a praying mantis once and kept it in a matchbox safely out of their sight for two days, but it died.

He didn't see many other children as they didn't have the money to pay for caravan park accommodation. Sometimes he got to play with other hippies' children at a music festival, but he was more interested in swapping something with them. He liked collecting books. He couldn't read until he was eight years old, but he liked the patterns of words and he liked to study the pictures. His favourite book was 'The Joy of Sex' although he did not understand any of it. His parents were free and easy about his education.

One day, before Byron turned eight, his parents decided to join a hippie hitchhiking adventure tour to Tibet. They explained to him they could not take him with them because he was too young and secondly, they did not have enough tins of chickpeas and green peas to make it to Tibet with all three of them.

His parents made the heart-breaking decision to drive little Byron up to Surfers Paradise to live with his mother's straightlaced parents, Vivienne and Bert. He never saw his parents again. They left in their kombi van, leaving behind his clothes, a pair of moccasins, his father's harmonica and a thick black plume of exhaust smoke. He cried for an hour after they left but then he was given a big bowl of strawberries and ice cream.

It was a vastly different life with this set of grandparents. For a start, their house was not on wheels and the scenery did not forever change. Their garden was full of fruit trees, cactus flower beds, cement ornaments and painted Australiana statues. And they cooked food instead of opening tins and tossing greens into a bowl. They even drove him down the road to meet a big bunch of other children who seemed to be partially controlled by adults and a big noisy bell which rang half a dozen times a day. This was called a school. It was here that he finally learnt to read and write. It opened a whole new world for him. Vivienne and Bert started calling him Phillip then. Little Phillip found that he really loved reading. He read everything he could get his hands on. Books, newspapers, women's magazines, comics, street directories, food wrappers, flyers, encyclopaedias and scientific papers. He even read his grandparents' prescriptions out loud to them. Early on they could see he was an excellent student and had a great memory.

Vivienne and Bert started up an education fund for Phillip as they were sure he would make it to university one day. And he did. He joined the police force when he left university with his law degree and quickly found out that he was a natural at profiling criminal types. He rose in the ranks with ease.

Sometimes, the grown-up Phil thought about his long-lost hippie parents. He wondered if they were alive out there somewhere. Maybe that was why he was drawn to the police force, and so good at investigative work. It was a secret yearning to learn the truth of what became of his parents someday.

Anyway, back to his date, he slapped on some stinky, very cheap aftershave because he had allergies to the expensive stuff and hopped into his white station wagon. He was a lover of routine. He did not like changing plans, so he wore the same clothes on all his dates and he knew exactly what he had to say.

Arriving early at the pub, he sat down in the far corner, on a plush red velvet couch where he could watch the door. He knew her name was Raquel and that she lived in a small town called Brumby Flat.

She arrived ten minutes later, fashionably late. Phillip recognised her straight away because profiling was so natural for him. She came in, after fumbling at the wrong door which was locked. A local would know which door to come through. She stood on the tips of her toes as if looking for someone. He noticed her face was wrinkle-free, her hair dyed blonde and tied back in a severe ponytail and she looked slim but top-heavy in her black jacket with matching skirt. She looked exactly like her dating app profile which surprised him. A lot of his dates were vastly different from their profiles. He didn't think she had a country girl look about her, but he accepted it was quite possible that she was a stylish exception, much like Grace Kelly.

He waved his hand casually. She spotted him. She tried not to show her disappointment by covering it up with an overbite smile. She did not like balding men.

He stood up to shake her outstretched hand. Raquel liked the fact that he was tall, standing at six foot two.

"Jason," he introduced himself confidently to her, "How are you?" his voice was strong and deep which she also liked.

"Raquel," she replied, "Very good, thanks. Lovely to meet you. How was your work-day?"

"Busy. It's not an easy shift when you must train a new security guard. Slows you up a bit. I just got home two hours ago. How was yours?"

"It was a flexiday so that was good. Worked ten minutes."

He indicated for her to take a seat on the red velvet couch, which she did. He sat next to her and took her hand gently into his. She was taken aback at such an early display of affection, mind you, his big hand was icy cold. He was looking deeply into her hazel eyes.

"You live a fair way away, in Brumby Flat," he made it sound like a question for her, "What's that like?"

Raquel took extra seconds to work out what she would say. She hadn't actually moved there yet, "Well, it's a typical small country town, I guess. Well, it appears to be. Very community-minded and everyone seems so friendly. I love the relaxed country lifestyle."

"Oh Okay. You wouldn't live in the city?"

"No, I moved into the country about seven years ago and I can't go back. The city traffic is such a headache, and the neighbours are far too close. Not my cup of tea. Love the country."

He clicked his tongue, "But if you had to live here again, where would you go?"

She flicked her head to one side and replied, "I guess…an apartment in the city, high up. That would be great. If I could see views of the hills and the parklands around me, that might be good. I like having views around me."

"I understand. I used to travel around the country. Quite a bit. I must be honest; I prefer living here. How often do you come into the city?"

"Not that often. Sometimes, when I need to."

"Tell me next time when you are here."

She thought it was an odd thing for him to say but nodded. She filled in an uncomfortable gap with a question herself, "How's your family? Do they all live here in Adelaide?"

Phillip had a standard answer for that. It always made his dates cosy up to him.

With a lump in his throat, he replied, "My parents died when I was very young and my grandparents who raised me…they have now passed away."

Raquel's eyes widened in surprise, "Oh, I am sorry to hear that. How awful."

He shrugged his shoulders, "I had a bit of an interesting childhood but my grandparents were wonderful, caring people."

"I have a small family, Just my mother, my son and myself. Oh yes, and my uncle too."

He did not react. His face was blank, unreadable.

"I have a surprise for you. Are you hungry?"

"Yes, definitely," she replied eagerly. She wondered which restaurant he was taking her to. There were restaurants and cafes up and down the road.

"I think you will like it. Do you like seafood, Italian, Mexican?"

"All of it."

He nodded and smiled very slightly, "You'll love the surprise. Come with me," he grabbed her hand firmly in his icy cold one and pulled her towards the front door. He stopped in the carpark, next to his station wagon.

"We have to drive a bit. We'll take my car."

Raquel raised an eyebrow at these words. She did not like the idea as he was a total stranger to her. For all she knew, he could be a serial killer. But then, she talked herself out of worrying as he was probably only driving her down the road, to the front of a restaurant door. It was, after all, an unusually chilly night.

She slid into his car and buckled up. She smiled at him but he did not return the smile. And he didn't turn into the main street. He turned left, into the back street. He drove through dimly lit side streets for three minutes and finally turned into a narrow driveway.

"This is my home," he said, "Tonight, I am cooking you a home-cooked meal."

Raquel felt cheated. If she wanted a home-cooked meal, she could've stayed at home and cooked one for herself. The fact that she drove two hours for a home-cooked meal, did not make her happy.

His home was very modern, with sleek lines. It was a narrow white townhouse surrounded by other narrow white townhouses. In the dim street lighting, they all looked the same to her. With some reluctance, she got out of his car and followed him to the front door which had a gated entrance. He locked the door behind her.

It was surprisingly spacious inside. It was a very conservative space which matched his conservative approach to fashion. She followed him into the open plan kitchen and family room at the back of the home. Once again, neat and conservative. She noticed he had left some paperwork on the dining table. She had just two seconds to take it in before he hastily picked it up and shoved it into a cupboard drawer. It looked like a couple of crime scene photos sticking partially out of a yellow manila folder.

"Okay, I'll start cooking. I hope you like seafood. In the meantime, you can make up a salad for us. Show us your culinary skills."

He opened his fridge and took out a plastic box full of vegetables and plonked a bottle of salad dressing onto the island bench. Then he gave her a giant carving knife to slice the vegetables with. He smiled briefly and then turned his back on her to start warming up the frying pan on the stove. Raquel held the long knife tight in her hand and admired it. Then she stared long and hard at his back, as he cooked the main meal. What if she was the serial killer, she thought to herself. How easy it would be to plunge the knife into his back in this unguarded moment.

She drew her focus back to the vegetables. She proceeded to slice and dice a good selection of the vegetables, although she felt more inclined to slice and dice his sausage. After drizzling the balsamic dressing over the salad and tossing it in a bowl, she realised this date was not working out for her.

"Jason," she said his name with a sharp tone which made him turn around immediately.

"Thank you very much for asking me out but this is…not what I had in mind. I did not see myself making a salad tonight. I wanted to go out to a restaurant."

He nodded as if he understood her concerns, "I thought you would appreciate a home-cooked meal."

"This is too much, too quick, too soon for me. I would like you to drive me back to the hotel. Sorry. I just want to go home. It's a really long way home, for me."

Jason, who was really Senior Detective Phillip Duncan, turned off the gas stove and looked uncomfortable. He was secretly shocked by her decision to leave.

He usually got past dinner at the dining table and got to at least kiss and fondle his date for the night on his leather three-seater lounge. Sometimes they stayed overnight for a bit of a toss in the hay. Sex was a great release from the pressures of his work. But this country girl wasn't going to play his little seduction game. It was not the outcome he had expected.

He walked her wordlessly to the front door and out into the cool night air. Not another word was exchanged between them.

He dropped her off at the pub and hoped he would never see her again. She was country; he was city, so he was confident that was it.

Raquel drove the long way home, into the frosty night, the car radio blaring away to keep her awake. She eventually left the twinkling lights of the city and chaotic traffic flow well behind her. It was not a date she wanted to particularly remember either. Maybe he was a serial killer she had safely escaped from. Or a suburban nutcase. At any rate, she decided to block him on her Facebook page and the dating app as soon as she got home.

Chapter Two

He had returned to the small town of Brumby Flat thirty-two years after he had left it. He had come back, a little naïvely perhaps, but had least expected the reception that he got. He did not see the blow coming. It came from behind him when he had turned his back on someone he had deemed trustworthy. He heard the smashing sound of bone and metal meeting together, rather than feeling it. He felt the unbelievable pain which accompanied the thunderclap sound a second after. He automatically lifted his right hand and felt very carefully the back of his head. A streaming torrent of liquid seemed to be running down his forehead and into his widened, fear gripped hazel eyes. His left hand was starting to visibly shake as he lifted it to his forehead and as his fingertips pulled away, he realised the liquid was actually warm red blood, his own warm red blood.

He fell down to his knees, feeling a weakening sensation. His hands and knees were resting on railway sleepers. The trains no longer ran, having stopped years ago. He was isolated as the railway station had long gone, pulled down and he was on the far edge of town, where only the grain silos were, standing white, tall and ominously high above him.

He felt another blow rain down upon him, this time, smashing across his right shoulder blade. He cried out and gasped out a heavy breath of pain.

"WHAT THE FUCK!!! WHAT ARE YOU DOING?" he shouted, but he was quietened by a swift blow to the right side of his mouth and jaw. He found he could no longer talk. His bottom jaw felt slack and didn't seem joined to his head anymore.

His survival instinct had started to set in. He began to crawl in the direction he thought Brumby Flat and civilisation was.

His trembling, bloodied hands pulled him along the steel railings of the track and his legs were struggling to push and half drag his body across the rotting timber sleepers. His breath was becoming more and more laboured and he could now see the blood gushing down his right shoulder. The pain was intense everywhere but he was managing to keep alert. He was willing himself not to blackout from the pain.

He heard two clear, definite footsteps on the sleepers behind him and he made a huge effort to turn his body over to face his assailant and if necessary, plead for his life. He turned in time to see the last blow swing at him. It smashed and splintered his face into the back of his head, He did not see the final part when the metal rod fatally ripped into his chest and his heart burst open. Blood flowed freely and spread across dry brown dirt, gravel and the railway sleepers.

After that, nothing. A great darkness followed.

His assailant turned killer hovered above his battered, bloody and broken body for a while, and perhaps planning their next gory mission. A short distance away, a murder of crows lining a tall gumtree 'cawed' out their own blood-curdling story against the dry and parched landscape.

****

It was a slow process moving into her new home in Brumby Flat. Raquel spent eight weeks packing up the house which amounted to over a hundred boxes, two big sheds full of stuff she couldn't even remember she had, three dining suites, five lounge suites and five beds. It seemed a task so impossible that the new purchasers organised the shed contents for her. They got the impression that if they didn't help her, they wouldn't be able to use the sheds to store their own stuff.

They waved her goodbye as the last trailer load left what was now their property. Actually, it had been their property in name for well over a month already, it is just that Raquel seemed rather slow to notice it. But they didn't want to upset her as she always appeared outwardly frazzled whenever she turned up, throwing a handful of boxes into her car.

The biggest challenge faced Raquel at the new home. Once again, she had to consider issues of space. The three dining suites, five lounge suites and five beds didn't exactly fit. Not to mention all the boxes. Half her worldly goods, most unpacked and unravelled, ended up thrown into the shop next door. Then she closed the door to forget it was even there. It took over that entire space too. She gradually brought boxes from the shop into the house but cupboards filled up quickly. Then she bought another dining suite locally which made things tighter again. She couldn't resist it as the tabletop had a white horse etched on it, which was perfect for Brumby Flat.

Raquel and her son were forced to jostle their way through narrow spaces around boxes and oversized furniture to get to places inside the house.

After ten straight days of negotiating these tight spaces, her son confronted her.

"This is so stupid. Raquel, I really think you have to make a decision."

"What was that, honey?" she asked her son.

"On this, all of this stuff. Do we really need, so much stuff?"

"I will deal with it one day, but not today. I need to find the time to work it out…what I can do with it all."

"Yeah, I have ideas for it," he grumbled.

"Okay, Okay, I promise you. I'll work on it tomorrow."

So as soon as she got up the next morning, she found a small scrap of paper and a pen and wrote, 'For Rent.'

She stuck it on one of the shops' front windows with a blob of blue-tack. That should finish her son's whinging and complaining. It would be a good excuse for her to tidy up and make room for a business to move in.

Then she decided she had better make an appearance at work. Raquel assumed her boss was probably missing her expertise.

But he wasn't. He could finally relax in his office and found some free time to play solitaire on his tablet PC and a few rounds of office golf. Ten days of no drama had done wonders for his nerves.

He heard her loud return and automatically propelled himself from his swivel chair. He mumbled something to his receptionist, saying he had a sudden client appointment and raced out the back door.

Raquel looked for him briefly and then disappeared into her office to make a series of personal phone calls. That kept her busy for three hours, then she was off home again.

"Have a good night," she yelled out, but there was no reply.

Another week had passed and Raquel had completely forgotten about placing her small 'For Rent' sign in the shop window.

She had just finished work and arrived home a bit earlier. She immediately threw her handbag onto the kitchen bench, ignored the housework which she had failed to tackle two weeks ago. She flicked the television remote to on. She settled in to watch a documentary on the life of bees for the early part of the evening.

She was quite surprised when she heard a loud, but definite and very persistent knocking on her front door. She opened it and immediately came face to face with a stylish lady two inches shorter than herself. She was about the same age as Raquel, probably in her late thirties. She had short bright auburn hair and the bluest of blue eyes Raquel had ever seen. They almost seemed unnaturally blue. She was very well dressed, in black flared trousers with a stylish red tartan wool shawl draped over a mint green linen top. The shawl was clipped tight in its place with a vintage pearl brooch. She was also holding a crochet black beret in her slight pale hand, rather than wearing it. She was holding nothing else, not even a handbag to match her stylish outfit.

"Hello, I read your sign in the window. You know, next door, in the shop window. I would love to rent your shop if it's still available," she said in a brisk, raspy but matter of fact voice.

Raquel had to think for a minute to catch up with what she was saying.

"Oh right, yes. You want to rent my shop. Who are you?"

"I'm Bette. Mrs Bette Mitchell. I live right on the edge of town, behind you. Well, there's a few of us involved with a small shop down the road, which I am renting. But it's really very small, I know for a fact that your shop is so much bigger, I think it's twice the size. I am looking to expand my stock, you see."

"Yeah hi, I'm Raquel."

"Yes, we know who you are. Raquel Willaston. We make it our business to find out who's new in our town." Bette smiled, her intense blue eyes twinkling in the sunlight.

"What sort of shop is it again? What do you sell?"

"Well, the shop is called 'Raindrops' and we stock umbrellas, gumboots, woollen hats, woolly scarfs, winter coats and rain jackets. We also have a small range of local community made goods. That's growing a little bit and then we are thinking about adding a café, maybe."

Raquel nodded, "Plenty of room here for that. So what's your offer, per week?"

Bette heaved a heavy sigh, "Well, I can't afford too much in rent. Our shop is a bit seasonal. It's run by me and a couple of local volunteers. I am paying sixty-five dollars a week where we are now. Are you okay with us paying the same to you?"

Raquel drifted off into her own world again. It was a bit of a shock to get someone interested in renting her shop.

"What? Sorry...How much?"

Bette's eyebrows knitted together, anticipating the worst, "Sixty-five per week for your shop."

"Okay. Done deal. When do you want to move in?"

"Should we have a coffee down at my shop and discuss it?"

Raquel nodded, "I'll get my coat."

She reached for her favourite long length leopard print coat behind the door and popped it over her work suit. She stepped out into the main street, locked her front screen door and noticed that Bette looked suitably impressed at her dress sense too.

Bette's shop was just at the other end of the street.

The lock proved difficult but Bette managed it after a minute of patient jiggling.

"I must get that fixed," she then changed her tune, "I guess we won't have to worry about it soon. Never mind."

They stepped inside, and Raquel noticed Bette's quirky sense of shop display and puzzling choice of merchandise. It was set up a bit like a market bazaar and oversized tables overflowing with goods dominated the space. There wasn't much room to move and Raquel found she had to jostle behind Bette to make it around the shop.

True to her word, Bette had umbrellas open and hanging down from the ceiling, raincoats of different sizes and colours adorning the walls and tables full of tarpaulins of various sizes, rainproof makeup and a row of gumboots. In one corner of the shop, she noticed the snow skiwear and a row of water skis. In another corner, she saw what she perceived as the community corner, with a small range of home-grown plants and herbs and some locally made postcards.

"Wow, you weren't kidding," Raquel exclaimed, "You are packed in tight here. Interesting shop but…I have to ask this, you know how you said it was a seasonal shop? Someone told me the other day that this is the second year of drought in the region. How do you sell any of this gear in your Raindrops Shop?"

Bette nodded her head, sighed heavily and fiddled with the pearl brooch on her tartan shawl.

"It's hard, doll. I can't afford to pay staff but I have a couple of great volunteers. I sell my umbrellas and rainwear probably two months of the year. I am on Facebook and I do have regular customers who come from the snowfields in Victoria every year. My snow gear goes but I did make a mistake with the skis. I ordered snow skis but I got water skis. This year, I also made a bit of a mistake ordering the snow gear. Unfortunately, they're all size eight or size eighteen. Sometimes, I sell about half a dozen umbrellas in summer too, as I tell everyone it's perfect to keep harmful UV rays away. Seems to work okay. Anyway, I've just bought myself some reading glasses so I can order the right stock for next year."

"Sounds hard. To keep this shop going, I mean."

Bette's large blue jay eyes welled up with tears. Over the next ten minutes, she told Raquel her brief life story to moving into Brumby Flat.

Bette and her husband Sandy (Sando for short) Mitchell had moved from Tasmania over two years ago. They had lived in a small coastal town near Port Arthur, where strangers rarely dared to stop in and if they did, the locals came outside to watch them from their verandas or peered quite visibly through their windows. Everyone there seemed to be a bit of a voyeur. And it seemed to rain ten months of the year. Bette described it as a bit of a miserable place.

Bette had a shop there too, selling exclusive ranges of umbrellas, raincoats and gumboots. It proved to be a good money spinner as the freezing high winds turned most umbrellas inside out within a couple of weeks, if not within days. In addition, there was a good tourist trade driving through, heading to Port Arthur.

One day, her Sandy came home early from work and rather excitedly told her that she should take her shop concept to the mainland. He had watched a documentary at his work, covering the beginnings of a lawnmower round franchise. They could do the same. He suggested they start a successful franchise and they could retire as millionaires. That evening, they had made all of their life-changing decisions. Sandy took a yellow pushpin, closed his eyes and pushed the pin into a map of mainland Australia. It landed on Brumby Flat in South Australia. They thought the rest of Australia would be as wet and woolly as Tasmania. So the Raindrops Shop was born.

They sold up their modest three-bedroom home on twenty acres and as they needed extra money to move, they also sold off their half share in a racehorse, which later went on to win the Melbourne Cup.

By the time they arrived in Brumby Flat and realised it was a place lucky to get rain for two months of the year, Bette had already ordered two years' worth of stock. She had confidently spent thirty-thousand dollars on stock and thousands on advertising and signage.

In Brumby Flat, they bought the only three-storey house around, built into the side of the only hill on the southern edge of town. They could not believe how cheap the house was. It had ten bedrooms, four bathrooms, two kitchens and two living areas. Sandy was happy as he had a three-car garage to tinker around in. Bette had toyed with the idea of opening a B&B in their new home but carting bed linen and ripe grapefruit up and down three flights of stairs for guests seemed too much work. Thankfully, she easily found an empty shop in the main street to rent.

Bette continued her short tale of woe, teary-eyed and eventually blurry-eyed. It wasn't long before she and Sandy worked out that the climate was not well suited to the business. In the first three months, the Raindrops Shop sold only two umbrellas, a tarpaulin and an inflatable life raft to an unexpected local. Sandy had to take up interstate truck driving again so they could live comfortably, feed their super spoilt Russian Blue cat named Pandora and Bette was forced to ask for volunteers to help her work the shop.

"Both Sandy and I are so lucky that we came here to Brumby Flat," Bette said, blowing her nose, "Everyone is friendly, and I have had so much support. The volunteers are fantastic and put in a hundred percent effort. Encouraging the community to buy umbrellas for a rainy day. Truly, they are amazing."

Raquel nodded her head, "So what was your plan again for my shop?"

"Well, if we have the room, I'd like to add a coffee shop and make extra money. With more money coming in, I can change the shop later on. Almost every week I get requests for chaps, whips or spurs. There's a rodeo not far away from here, so I think that's what I might need to sell."

"Oh, I see. Will be a bit of a change."

"Yes, but I do need to survive financially, and the town needs to grow too."

"So what's the deal here?"

"The deal is…I might rent your shop out but it must be fair. I can't afford high overheads."

Raquel rolled her eyes, "Well, I don't know. There's a lot of moving stuff around I have to do…"

"We'll help you move it."

"And maybe I came out here to find peace and quiet. Maybe I don't want to socialise much."

Bette peered at her with her piercing blue jay eyes. Finally, she said, "Well, doll, you do have to be careful in Brumby Flat. There are two camps living here. I like to think I am one of the new guards with new ideas. But there are people who have lived in this town all their lives. Now they are the type of people who could easily bet on two flies climbing up a wall, and then there's the type who will pick the wings of a fly without blinking an eyelid. No. You don't want to make enemies here. You learn to get along or you'd best just leave town."

Raquel shrugged her shoulders, "Okay. What are you telling me…?"

"All I am saying is that you put 'For Rent' in your shop window. And here I am. I have ideas and I hope you accept my offer to rent the space."

"Bette, you have yourself a shop. I said it's okay."

She smiled broadly and beckoned to the coffee machine in the corner, "Wow, thank you. I don't have a proper bottle of bubbly to share, but I did promise you a coffee. Let's celebrate, doll."

Raquel did not say no. She lived on at least six cups of coffee every day. Bette proved to be good with the expensive coffee machine and made her a perfect soy milk chai latte. They sat down or rather perched on two very rickety outdoor chairs which were designed for decoration rather than for practical use.

Raquel and Bette talked away for the next two hours, losing track of time. Conversation came easily between them and at the end of their time together that evening, Raquel realised that she had found herself a new good friend. Bette was around the same age but seemed to be wise on all things. She had only lived in Brumby Flat for two years yet she knew everyone in town. She knew who was rich, who was a bit strange, who was arty and who was to be avoided at all cost. She knew all the town gossip too, and Raquel was both suitably impressed and enthralled.

"Oh, and you'll find the towns biggest bitch and loosest woman working over there in the post office. You can't trust your husband or boyfriend around her. I make sure my Sandy doesn't ever go in there. I hear so many stories about Bridie, so beware. Keep your son away from her too. What's his name, doll?"

Raquel had to think a moment, "Steve."

Bette nodded her head enthusiastically, still clutching her stone-cold cup of coffee, "Have to be careful of Bridie. She's broken up seven marriages in town that I am aware of."

"Oh wow. Is there anyone else I should steer clear of?"

Bette rolled her eyes in thought, "No. Mind you, we might have a cat among the pigeons when Phillip C. Proctor comes to town in two weeks."

She sipped her coffee and made a disagreeable face.

"Who's he?"

Bette raised an eyebrow, "You really don't know?" she exclaimed.

Raquel shrugged her shoulders, "No idea. I'm sorry."

"Well. He's just the best Silo painter in the world. Our town's paid for it. It took the community about five years –

they raised a lot of money with cake stalls, chocolate drives and lemonade stands. And Girl Guide cookies. Everyone in town put on weight. I put on three kilos I reckon. I've lost it now, thank goodness. Anyway, Phillip Proctor is coming over from New York to paint what our town is famous for."

"A brumby, brumbies," Raquel cried out.

"No. Goats. We have the best goat cheese around."

"Oh wow…of course." Raquel remembered she had seen a big paddock full of goats somewhere nearby.

"The painted silos will bring people into town, to look at the mural by Proctor. Apparently, he's very eccentric and a bit of a temperamental genius. Just like most artists, I suppose. He's going to put our Brumby Flat on the map."

Raquel simply nodded her head in agreement.

Chapter Three

Bette had her job cut out for her with the Raindrops Shop. All of her three shop volunteers were very different in persona and outlook. They were also 'outsiders' in town for various reasons.

Anabella Jilly Williams nee Sawyer was the first one who had approached Bette to help in the shop. She was on the verge of turning seventy, but life for her had hardly changed in the last forty-five years. She could be easily spotted walking about in the district. She grew up in the nineteen-fifties, so being comfortable in that era, she never left her house without her white gloves on, her large wicker basket in hand, the petticoats, the swing skirts and her twin sets in an array of rainbow colours. Her hair was set and sprayed into place every week at the local hairdresser's. Her thick brown hair was now salt and peppered, but she still retained her slim waistline and her swing dancing ability, two attributes she was extremely proud of.

Anabella had lived in Brumby Flat all her life and she lived in the past due to a personal tragedy which happened forty-five years ago.

In her twenties, she was a gifted tennis player and met her future husband at the local dance and on the tennis court. He was only ten years older than her and very fit. It was the late nineteen-sixties but Anabella preferred to look very prim and proper when she stepped out, inspired by her parents' generation. Which attracted Bruce Williams immediately to her. He liked the way she carried herself like a model sprung from the pages of the Australian Women's Weekly, which she read cover to cover every week.

She would flounce down the main street of Brumby Flat in her gingham or floral swing dresses propped with tulle and lace petticoats, wearing her dainty white gloves, cats eye sunglasses, kitten heels and vinyl handbag poised high on her right wrist. She stood out from the farmers' wives coming to town to order their metres of Crimplene fabric and strands of black pom-poms at the local drapery.

It took some time for Bruce to summon enough courage to ask Anabella's conservative parents for her hand in marriage. The town seemed to rejoice when it finally happened. Anabella was something of an oddity in town, an outsider. She was not interested in the new mod 'sixties groups and their pop music. Or the 'sixties fashion where hemlines were high and hair was piled even higher.

Anabella and Bruce had a few dates before their wedding. He was very romantic and attentive to her needs. He made her feel like a princess so she easily fell in love with him.

She went into Adelaide to specially pick out her wedding dress and her honeymoon outfit. She picked out a tea-length white dress with a sweetheart neckline and finished off with a short lace frilled jacket. Instead of a tulle veil, she chose a wide satin ribbon to tie up her long luxurious hair in a ponytail.

Her honeymoon dress was mint green in colour with a wide black vinyl belt to emphasise her tiny waist, pleated skirt with little cap sleeves. She found the perfect black beret to give her a distinctly French look which was currently in vogue. Bruce had arranged their honeymoon in the Riverina, in regional New South Wales, which she thought would be exactly like the French Riviera. She packed her one-piece bathing suit just in case she had a chance to sunbathe.

Their wedding was the event of that year in the township. After the wedding, they drove straight to their reception at the local town hall. It was here that Anabella's life was changed forever.

Anabella and Bruce were in the midst of their bridal waltz when Bruce let her dainty white-gloved hands go and spun around, eyes wide as he clutched his chest and then fell face down into the reception cake, which Anabella had made herself. They were fortunate to have the town's physician in attendance, but he looked briefly at Bruce after they turned him over and removed most of the icing. He had the unfortunate task to explain to a hysterically upset Anabella that Bruce had died instantly from a massive heart attack. Suffocation from the dense icing sugar was possibly a secondary cause.

Anabella was heartbroken and inconsolable. She did not leave her parents' home for the next four years. When she finally emerged, the world had changed quite dramatically again. Man had walked on the moon and women's fashion was hippie style, with lots of bright prints and flared trousers. She now had a difficult time adjusting to the new world. She continued to get her hair set and styled as she had in the past, and she still flounced around town in her cute swing dresses.

She gave up her tennis because it reminded her of playing competition with Bruce. She was a great cook but she could not even sew a button so she had to keep looking for nineteen-fifties dresses to buy. They were at first classed as 'old fashioned', found easily in Op Shops and eventually, they became highly prized vintage wear at specialised preloved fashion boutiques. At this turning point, she was forced to sometimes pay out two hundred dollars or more for a vintage piece. Or else, pay even more money to purchase beautiful fabric and a dressmaker's skills. Her parents had passed away two decades earlier but she still lived in their home, which looked like a nineteen-fifties museum.

Over the years she had met a couple of men who wanted to date her, but she refused. She still loved Bruce and kissed his faded photograph on her dressing table every morning.

At the Raindrops Shop, she escaped routine for a little while, but she still talked to people about her husband Bruce, as if he was living and breathing. Bette was concerned at first. After a while, she relaxed, as Anabella was very stylish and could sell an umbrella as soon as she twirled it in her white-gloved hands. She also made killer cakes.

The next volunteer was Chris Jones. He was an ex-military officer and Bette sometimes found him hard to take. Not much was known about his life before Brumby Flat. He arrived in town ten years ago and he was also easy to spot. He only wore army fatigues from army surplus stores and he lived his life by his watch.

With military-like precision, he presented himself at the post office, the Butcher and the Hardware store every day on the hour. His home too reflected his strict military training. He had planted neat rows of miniature roses, petunias and forget-me-nots in his front garden. Footpaths were built straight and squared perfectly.

On his shifts at the Raindrops Shop, he would spend considerable time polishing umbrella handles and anything else liable to shine. If he was working with anyone else, including Bette, he would shout out instructions. If people came into the shop, he would escort them and have them 'march' in an orderly fashion up and down the narrow aisles.

Bette was relieved when another volunteer stepped up to the plate. Cindy Mayland tapped quietly on the shop window one day when Bette was inside after she had just closed the shop. Cindy was an ex-primary school librarian who had suffered a nervous breakdown two years ago, caused by noisy out of control school children. She barely said a word. In most cases, it was a game of charades to work out what she wanted to tell people. If you were lucky, she would whisper or mumble close to your ear and some of her words would be audible.

Cindy was short and painfully thin. Her hair was mousey, limp and often greasy and her clothes were two twenty-year-old maroon tracksuits she washed and cleaned every second day. She never wore makeup and her sensible choice of footwear was leather school shoes because her feet were so tiny. She had trouble doing up her shoelaces so she just knotted them a couple of times and cut off the excess.

When Raquel came to the Raindrops Shop to officially meet the volunteers, before the big move into her larger shop, she was surprised by the diversity of the staff. She was greeted by Anabella who was powdered up and dressed in her best new vintage blue floral dress with a bright pink cardie, complete with cream gloves and pale blue kitten heels. Then there was a standing-at-attention Chris proudly outfitted in his best camouflage gear and Cindy looking very small, nervous and childlike in one of her faded maroon tracksuits. Bette was a clothes horse, as usual, dressed in a predominately red tartan skirt teamed with a black short-sleeved T-shirt and a string of pearls. Anabella often chastised women who wore pearls before five o'clock in the afternoon.

Bette made coffees for everyone and Anabella had made pinwheel sandwiches and pumpkin scones for morning tea. No customers had turned up so far as the shop was open for business. The staff settled down to enjoy coffee and indulge in shop talk which lasted about ten minutes. Cindy just nodded. The dialogue cut off as Bette looked through the shop windows and up at the sky. Her blue jay eyes widened.

"Oh my god. Incoming!" she cried out in her raspy voice.

"What on earth…?" Raquel whirled around in the swivel chair she had been provided.

All the volunteers shot up out of their chairs and raced outside. Raquel didn't know what to do or what was happening until Bette pointed at the sky which had turned blood red. It was a huge whirling dust storm bearing down on Brumby Flat. Outside, the wind was starting to pick up. The umbrellas which were decorating the outside veranda were starting to roll across the pavement and down the street. Chris had put out thirty and the ladies were struggling to save them all. The wind was lifting Anabella's petticoats as she rescued an umbrella with one gloved hand and she had to hold down her floral skirt with the other.

But Cindy had it much tougher as she was smaller and lighter in stature. She was really struggling to keep her feet literally on the ground. As soon as she had an open umbrella in her hand, she would lose her balance. Chris came running and saved her as she was stumbling towards the main road. He could tell she was in trouble as she was posturing like a mime artist.

"Cindy, go inside now. I'll handle this," he barked at her in his usual military style. Cindy was very afraid of him so obeyed immediately.

Bette ran out of the shop and rescued two more umbrellas which were twirling around like circus performers on the vacant lot next door. She could not afford to have damaged stock sitting around in her shop. Raquel followed her outside a minute later. They had a very short time to save the umbrellas, which were rolling or flying around. The dust storm was nearly ready to engulf the township. It would be an unfortunate turn of events for the local farmers, who were barely coping with the two-year drought.

"Quick, get inside," Bette yelled out above the whistling wind.

The red dust was starting to get into their eyes so it was a good time to give up a hopeless fight. Bette, Raquel, Chris and Anabella returned to the safety of the shop, latching the front door securely behind them.

Doors, windows rattled and anything not tied down flapped around in the high wind. Through the windows, the dust swirled around the main street and the skyline was tinged with red.

Bette shook her head and cast apologetic glances to all, "I am sorry but we'll have to stay here for a couple of hours. These dust storms are pretty bad up here, Raquel. Since the drought started, we've had a number of them," she said.

Chris spoke up, "I think we've lost a few umbrellas to the elements, Liz," he said in his usual sharp tone of voice.

Bette visibly frowned. She didn't understand why Chris persisted with calling her Liz when he already knew her name was just plain old Bette.

"Never mind. It's funny when you think about it."

Raquel looked at her new friend, an eyebrow raised, "Why?"

"Umbrellas dotted randomly in a landscape, doll. Could be the new town mural."

Cindy was the only one who reacted to the image. She barely said a word but at this, she smiled and allowed herself to make a very small chuckling sound in the back of her throat.

****

Phil Proctor had arrived in Brumby Flat two days before. Now he was walking around the perimeter of the town's silos, to become familiar with his new major project. He had been picked up at Adelaide Airport by an overenthusiastic Bette Mitchell and her husband whose name he thought was Sando. By the time they got within the outskirts of his new home for the next twelve months, Proctor had been well educated in Australian small township etiquette and the local gossip during that long drive. He was also excited to see his first real kangaroo. As their SUV slowed down to sixty kilometres, a large red kangaroo appeared out of the trees and hopped effortlessly alongside the vehicle, before veering off onto the road verge.

The town had provided him with his own farmhouse and twenty acres to enjoy, completely rent-free. An added bonus was the black thoroughbred mare he had found 'parked' in the stables. He thought she was a real beauty and he had already spent some time half whispering to her, feeding her and rubbing her down. As soon as the jet lag left him, he was going to ride her. At sixty-six, he found it took longer to relax and shake off the jetlag.

He found the whole town interesting. The sign outside of Brumby Flat stated it had a population of two hundred and fifty-one people. There wasn't a lot to it. In the main street, most people lived in the shops. There was a post office, a service station on the corner, run by a Nigerian couple who were new migrants and spoke very little English but they knew the colour of money, and the oddly named Raindrops Shop which seemed to be in the process of a big shift.

Proctor looked relaxed in his chambray shirt and favourite Levi's jeans and the new Rossi boots he had bought from the Raindrops Shop, as he trudged across the hot mix of gravel, sand and shrubs. He remembered reading somewhere that Australia had the plainest but deadliest snakes in the world. Therefore, he started to make sure he was not walking too close to the saltbush.

Proctor looked up at the silos, his pale but penetrating blue eyes squinting in the strong midday sunlight. He swept a hand through his silver-grey thick hair. He estimated the silos were over thirty metres high. He did think it was strange that they were not positioned where they would be seen and admired by people when the mural was done. The railway had evidently closed down years ago and the road access was blocked off by two large concrete barriers. He couldn't understand why they wanted a goat mural either. He would have preferred to paint a herd of wild horses, using his on-loan black mare as a model. But he wasn't going to argue about the money they were paying him to do the project. He had not yet been updated that the local council had already voted on building a new traffic bypass road past the silos.

He had nearly finished his walk around the perimeter of the silo, turning the corner and leaving the railway tracks behind him. Suddenly, he thought he heard a noise, other than bird song. He looked wildly behind him but saw nothing moving. Maybe it was a lizard or snake crossing the sand and weaving its way through low shrubs. Although Proctor thought it had sounded more like faint, distant footsteps.

As he turned the last corner finally, an awful stench hit him. He visibly flinched and quickly covered his nose. He saw a dead blue tongue lizard near his feet, but he knew that couldn't possibly be the source. The lizard's scaly grey carcase was all that was left, as ants and other small creatures had entered through its broken tail and devoured its insides.

Then Proctor saw what it really was. There was a fresh mound of dirt mixed with sand, just raised slightly, and as he walked closer to it, he was sure he could see a torn piece of clothing protruding from it. He leaned in for a closer look and then quickly pulled away. He had seen more than he had wanted to see. It looked like part of a human hand was just visible above the dirt.

"Oh shit, goddamn it," he exclaimed loudly.

He reacted instantly, without thinking and just reached into his jeans pocket for his mobile phone, which he called a cell. Bette had told him that triple 'o' was the 911 emergency call number in Australia.

It took only a few seconds, "Hello? Police? Yes, I want the local police. Closest to Brumby Flat."

A few more seconds passed before he had the right connection.

"Yeah, howdy. I am staying in a small town called Brumby Flat. I reckon…there's been a murder up here. I'm just standing here at the grain silos, and there's a body. It looks like a body," he said to the female police officer on the other end of the line, "No, I don't wanna get any closer, ma'am."

"My name? Sure thing. Phillip C. Proctor. I'm an artist here. I've come over from the states."

"Sure, I'll stay put. But kind of hurry," he looked nervously at the dry landscape around him, "I am out here, alone."

"Ten minutes away? Okay. I'm standing at the back of the silos, behind the old railway tracks. Thanks, ma'am."

Proctor finished the call, and now wished he hadn't wandered up here on his own. He believed he was half a kilometre from the edge of the town. The stench in the air was terrible and blowflies were circling and swooping everywhere around him.

Fifteen minutes passed quickly and he felt a great sense of relief when he clearly heard a police siren in the distance, getting ever closer and louder. He was not looking forward to the questioning process.

Chapter Four

He was walking along the country road verge, hoping to hitch just one more ride. He knew he was close. Not far from Brumby Flat which was to be his final destination. He estimated he had forty kilometres left to go. It had been a long trip from where he had started his journey from, on the outskirts of Townsville. He was dirty and a bit on the nose. He had limited opportunities to shower or wash along the way. His worldly goods were tucked away in his backpack. Because shaving was difficult and random, he had grown a small beard peppered with grey and his curly brown hair was matted and messy. He was dressed in a red and orange check long sleeve flannel shirt which had seen better days, teamed with dusty, faded jeans. His well-worn Doc Martens boots, given to him by a kind stranger, were getting harder to walk in. When it rained, water seeped through the holes in his boots. But looking around at the landscape now, he didn't remember the area ever being so dry.

He was used to living out of a backpack. For the last ten years, he had been living rough, on the streets of Newcastle. Not by his choice. He had fallen on hard times for a while and by the time he had negotiated his way through it, he had grown accustomed to living that way.

It was a difficult decision he made to return to Brumby Flat after thirty-two years in exile. He had some unfinished business to take care of.

He could see a white car coming up behind him, coming up rather fast over the hill. He put his thumb up and hoped this driver would stop. Most people drove by because he looked like trouble. The fact that he was a middle-aged man, alone, with a backpack seemed a dangerous enough proposition.

The car was an early nineteen-eighties white station wagon which looked as unwashed as he did. The car slowed down as it neared him and he started to feel a sense of relief. It pulled to a dead stop right next to him, and the driver leaned over and wound down the passenger window. An old farmer smiled back at him. His face was grey and lined like a road map. He was wearing faded blue denim overalls.

"Where you headed, mate?" he said to the hitch-hiker.

"Not far. Just need a ride into Brumby Flat."

The old cocky nodded his head and winked, "Righto. That's where I am going to. C'mon, jump in but put your bag in the back, thanks."

After a couple of moments, he climbed into the passenger seat and settled in for the last ride.

They were both quiet, watching the road unfurl for the next five kilometres before the old farmer spoke.

"You look a bit familiar. I reckon you have any family in town?"

The hitch-hiker shook his head, "No. I am just visiting, looking up an old friend."

"Oh yeah? Who? I probably know 'em. Lived in Brumby Flat all me life."

The stranger moved uncomfortably in the passenger seat and replied quite firmly, "It's going to be a surprise, you know?"

The farmer nodded in understanding and went back to just driving.

After twenty minutes, a high canopy of huge gumtrees appeared, looming large over the road, and an eighty-kilometre speed sign indicated they were about to drive into town. The stranger noticed more dirt and sand with thin patches of grass as they drove under the canopy of tree branches which were just holding onto their last winter leaves.

"Can you please drop me off at the post office?"

"Yep. Sure thing, mate."

The farmer slowed down and stopped where the stranger had indicated. He retrieved his backpack from the back of the vehicle.

"Thanks mate," the hitch-hiker waved him goodbye, He slung his backpack over his left shoulder and looked around, trying to get his bearings. It had been thirty-two years. He stood still for a few minutes. He soon realised that the post office was now in another building than what he had remembered and half the shop fronts in the main street were now closed with people living in them. Then he turned west, into the side street behind the new post office. He was sure it was the right way.

According to his battered old watch, it was thirty-five past five pm daylight saving time and his arrival into town had certainly not gone unnoticed.

Bette Mitchell was in her old shop, dusting now empty shelves. She saw the stranger emerge from the white station wagon, and she wondered what a homeless person was doing in Brumby Flat. That's how he looked to her. But she had only paused for a few seconds, and then returned to her dusting.

Across the other side of the main street, another person experienced the newcomer's arrival as well. They were hiding in the shadows. They were exposed for only a second or two and then merged with the darkness before they became recognisable.

That someone followed the stranger all the way down that street to his eventual destination. Less than twelve hours later, the stranger would be dead.

****

It did not take long for the news to spread throughout the town. Everyone was talking about it. Phil Proctor had stumbled across a dead body by the silos. At least four people so far had admitted to seeing a stranger in town the night before the discovery of the body. The consensus was that he was a poor unfortunate homeless man who had met with foul play. And his killer could not possibly be a local.

Chaos now reigned but Bette Mitchell was profiting the most from it. Her Raindrops Shop was very suddenly busy making teas and coffees for all the newspaper reporters, the police and the detectives who had descended upon the town. Anabella was enjoying it too as her killer cakes and fruit custard vol-au-vents were selling well. Raquel even took a week off from her hectic job to get a handle on what was going on around her. When her boss found out, he took leave off as well and went straight up to the Gold Coast, chasing the sun but not the heat. He spent most of his time up there sitting in air-conditioned bars and restaurants.

Raquel could see all the action was happening in Bette's shop so she quickly put on her favourite leopard print skirt and a cream shirt and lightly hair sprayed her blonde hair. She was really hoping to bump into Phil Proctor. He sounded rather intriguing to her.

She walked outside and straight into her shop next door. Bette and her helpers had done an amazing job. The front two rooms were set up so far with colourful umbrellas and snow skis already and the cafe part was off and running. Inside the rectangular long room, Bette had three round café tables with chairs lined down the middle.

"Wow. Looks fabulous in here. I like what you've done to your hair too," Raquel said, greeting her friend who was busy working the hissing, splattering and frothing coffee machine. As usual, Bette was dressed her clothes horse best. Her auburn hair was cut high to the nape of her slender, pale neck and she was wearing a pastel linen dress with a V-neck embroidered floral detail.

"Ah, doll," Bette winked at her, "I'm glad to see you. Got some people I have to introduce to you. They're just looking around in the other room."

Raquel's heart appeared to leap up into her throat. She really hoped it was Proctor. She was getting tired of hearing all about him. He was like a phantom, but she was sure he was pretty real.

She heard a couple of strong male voices coming closer.

Bette smiled at Raquel, "Here they are. I'd like to introduce you to Detective Phillip Duncan and Detective Longmeil."

Raquel spun around and her smile gradually faded away when she recognised him. Standing at six foot two, his bright blue eyes widened behind his glasses and then narrowed to slits when he saw her. He was dressed in a conservative brown suit, but there was no hiding the shaved, nearly no hair situation, plus she remembered his cheap smelling aftershave.

"Jason," Raquel snorted, her eyes narrowing as well.

"I'm Senior Detective Phillip Duncan."

"No, you're not. You're Jason and you're a security guard."

He shifted from one foot to another uncomfortably, "I assure you that I am Senior Detective Phillip Duncan," he repeated, at a lower tone of voice, then he added in near panic mode, "Oh my god. Crap. This is Brumby Flat, isn't it? Of course. You said you lived in Brumby Flat."

"Okay, well…I see," Raquel drew out her words too and kept staring back at him. She stood still, her left hand by her side clenching into a fist. She was very angry with him but she had to admit his piercing blue eyes were hard to ignore.

There was a very long uncomfortable silence before Bette finally decided to pipe up in her raspy voice, "Well, isn't this very nice, and rather cosy. You two obviously have a lot to talk about. We'll leave you to it." She turned on her heel and went back to the coffee machine. She was expecting a couple of newspaper reporters who had jumped on her app and pre-ordered their two soy milk chai lattes.

Detective Longmeil also retreated and was not seen for at least ten minutes.

The silence and intense face-off between the two of them continued for another half a minute.

Raquel finally spoke, "I can't believe this. You are so, so fake, Jason. Why are you doing this?"

He took a short intake of breath, "Oh god. I already told you. I am really a Senior Detective from Adelaide. I'm over here in relation to the murdered man. I am sure you've heard something about it. It's all over the news."

"You mean, you lied to me, on *our* date?"

He shrugged his broad shoulders, "Everyone lies on these dating sites and apps. You're a big girl. You should know that," he replied with a smirk.

"Shit. I was completely honest with you. So you're not who you said you were…to me."

He shook his head, "No. Look. Anyway, let's build that bridge and just get over it. Rachel, isn't it?"

"No. My name is Raquel, I am Raquel."

"Of course. Yep, I remember. Now, this man's body was found two days ago at the silos. Did you speak to or see this gentleman in town?"

"Are you really serious? Now, you want to change the subject."

"I need to question people in town. It is my job, as a detective."

Raquel shook her head, rolled her eyes and backed away from him, "You're unbelievable."

Before he had a chance to say anything else, she walked off, heading to the front door of the shop. Senior Detective Duncan did not know what to do. He just rolled his shoulders and resolved to ask her some questions at a later time, when she had chilled out. He had other people in town to question anyway.

In the meantime, Raquel was standing outside on the shop veranda, looking out over the street, people watching. She saw a tall man in the distance, heading towards the direction of the post office with a purposeful stride. He had a confident swagger about him which immediately drew her attention.

"Proctor," she half-whispered to herself.

No! NO! NO! She cursed loudly in her mind when she saw Phil Proctor open the creaky door and disappear inside the post office across the street.

"Damn it, that would be right," she sighed. As far as she knew, from what she had heard, this man-eater named Bridie would make mincemeat out of him.

She was, of course, right.

It was Phil Proctor, and Bridie did notice him as much, if not more than Raquel. The provocative ladies perfume he was wearing caused her to turn around sharply behind her tall counter. Her counter was partially covered in boxes and parcels which were still awaiting sorting and collection. There were notices overlapping and plastered all over the timber counter surfaces. Not to mention the layer of dust. Bridie, as a rule, did not like house cleaning duties when there were other far more exciting things to do. Moreover, sometimes she was more interested in the male of the species than actually sorting the mail.

Proctor had noticed the general state of untidiness and all the dried-up fly and moth corpses lined up on her shopfront windowsill. He tried not to dwell on this vision as the murder scene he came across two days earlier was still very fresh in his mind. The police had questioned him for five long hours that day.

Bridie gave him her best welcoming smile, "Well. Hello. You're wearing Red Door. I love Red Door," she drank in his rough edges but handsome features.

"Yes, ma'am." His American drawl immediately excited her.

Bridie was not attractive, being a bit of a plain Jane. But she was big on personality and her figure was trim. She had shoulder-length brown curly hair which was hard to tame. Her hazel eyes were spaced too far apart, her cheeks were often rosy, her nose slightly too big with tight, pinched nostrils and a mouth wide and pouty. She didn't wear much makeup and she wasn't a clothes horse either. Her style was plain, simple and uncomplicated. She was wearing a sleeveless black T-shirt that day, teamed with her favourite skinny jeans.

"Bloody hell! I've heard all about you. You're that famous mural painter, Proctor from New York," she exclaimed.

"Yeah, you got me there," he winked at her, taking in her easy smile and her pert looking breasts which he could just see heaving over the top of the shop counter.

"Hey there. I'm Bridie Browne. It's Browne with an 'e'," she put out her tanned hand, which he shook very firmly, "Lovely to meet you. Are you expecting something to come in, post wise?"

He replied in his harsh whisper of a voice, "Um, post wise, I ordered some paint, charcoal and butchers' paper before I arrived. I thought it might be here by now."

"Proctor? No, nothing has arrived for you, not yet anyway. But there may be another parcel delivery in about an hour."

Bridie hopped down somewhere behind the counter so Proctor assumed she had been perched high on a stool. She suddenly appeared through a doorway to Proctor's right. She stood pleasingly at his chest height when she finally confronted him.

"It's lunchtime, so I'm just going to close the post office."

Proctor looked briefly down at his watch, "It's only eleven in the morning."

She smiled up at him in a teasing way, "Yes, I know. Perhaps we can get to know each other. We've got, like, an hour all to ourselves."

She latched the front door, pulled the dusty and fragile nineteen-seventies burnt orange curtains over the shop windows and brushed up against him with her breasts. He leaned in and could smell the heady scent of her perfume, the apple shampoo in her hair and the lavender-scented hand cream she wore. He started to breathe a bit harder and just a little bit faster.

"Are we likely to be disturbed?"

She shrugged her shoulders, "Only if you have a jealous girlfriend or wife chasing you. I hope you haven't got any one of those."

He moved in closer and traced the round arc of her left breast with his right index finger to her hard nipple as she pressed her lithe body longingly into his. She raised her hazel eyes and full pouty lips to him. He studied her with his intense blue eyes and she reached out to touch his experienced face. His left hand very gently touched her soft, pale neck and drew her lips closer to his own. He kissed her softly and increased the intensity slowly and Bridie yielded to his every touch.

"Mr Proctor," she purred, "I don't think we should stop."

He smiled back at her, "I had no intention to, Lil' Missy."

He kissed her again, a little bit harder this time. He kept kissing her and didn't miss a heartbeat even as he lifted her black T-shirt over her head. She stood before him, half-naked, her chest heaving and he dutifully removed his shirt too. He could see she was much younger than he was, only in her mid-thirties but he found her too exciting to walk away from. He hardly expected to find so much fun in the small town of Brumby Flat and so fast. Especially in the local post office. Someone rattled the front door, trying to get in but they took no notice.

"Whoa, cowboy," she said in a low, seductive tone, the palms of her hands softly resting on his chest, "Enough of your kisses. Kisses are a bit too intimate for me."

Proctor could feel his erection pressing hard inside his Levi's. He did not need to reach for Viagra today. The only drawback was the lack of a couch around or another soft piece of furniture to enjoy sex on. He wasn't exactly a young Lothario anymore and craved some comfort these days.

Bridie seemed to have read his mind and lifted an index finger to press against his lips.

"I'll be right back. Got a nice surprise for you," she said, "I've been looking forward to using it actually."

She raced into the backroom, her pert breasts with pink nipples jutting out like raisins, swinging gently. She returned seconds later with a plastic carry case in hand.

"Stand right back," she warned him, leaning over and opening the case and tugging on a cord. Within seconds, a lot of hissing and a fully inflated rubber life raft appeared ready to use, with room enough to hold six people adrift on an ocean far away from a drought-stricken small town.

Proctor gasped and laughed at the same time.

"Isn't this great. I bought it from that crazy weird Raindrops Shop across the road. Not a drop of water anywhere but I saw it and I knew it would be useful one day."

"Whatever floats your boat, I suppose," he said with a wry smile, "Well. Yeah, I'll have to go and check out what they have in that fancy store over there."

She quickly unzipped her skinny jeans. They fell with a thud onto the dusty shop floor. Proctor dutifully removed his Levi's and there was no hiding his erect well-proportioned penis. They jumped into the life raft together and it was a bit like an adults-only bouncing castle. Whenever they moved and tried another position, the raft creaked, squeaked and smacked loudly against their naked skin. A couple of times, they heard someone knocking on the front door. It sometimes sounded like someone was shouting. But they didn't care.

Proctor shuddered in ecstasy as Bridie sat on top of him, grinding her hips and sliding up and down expertly on his agreeable, rock hard cock. He came first, gasping deep within his throat and she came screaming blue murder very soon after him. She was so loud he had to cup his right hand over her mouth. Damn, he thought to himself. I had to find myself a screamer. He firmly slapped her left butt cheek at the end and she squealed out in delight.

They sat back, on opposite ends of the life raft, sweating, flushed in the heat of the moment and staring hard at each other.

"Wowee, cowboy," Bridie licked her lips, "That was bloody fun."

Proctor nodded his response. He was too exhausted to react in any other way.

A couple of minutes passed before another word was said.

"We should do it again one day. Soon-ish. Hey, how old are you, Proctor?"

"I'm sixty-six, ma'am."

"Shit! Really? You're the oldest man I've had a fuck with," she exclaimed, her hazel eyes narrowing then widening, "But you're damn good value, cowboy."

Five minutes passed and then Proctor got up to stretch his arms and retrieve his jeans. He then made the mistake of pulling them up inside the life raft and his lucky pocketknife fell out of his Levi's back pocket. The knife bounced, opened up and then ripped a tear into the raft and Bridie gasped in horror. Proctor reclaimed his knife quickly and tucked it back into his back pocket.

"Gosh. Sorry about that."

A topless Bridie raced into the back room looking for the repair kit. The life raft was deflating slowly and she realised she had no time to patch the tear. She needed to open the front door soon for the next big parcel delivery. The raft was taking up a lot of shop floor space.

"Thanks, Bridie," he said in his harsh whisper tone, "I'll see you around."

She nodded briefly, "Use the backdoor over there. Thanks."

He left her to deal with her conundrum.

Proctor walked out and securely closed the door behind him. He was a bit disappointed that she had ignored him after their athletic sex session, which left him wondering how many lovers she had in this small town. He decided it might be best to stay away from her in future unless she made her interest in him quite clear. He had been around the block several times and then some. However, when it came to love, intimacy and relationships, he was still a sensitive man. He was still looking for perfect love.

His first marriage had been a disaster. He played high school football and the lead cheerleader with her baby blue peepers, blond bangs and long legs immediately caught his eye. They married at eighteen and had their only child, a boy they named Jonathon, twelve months later. They were too young and neither of them stayed faithful. Five years later, they separated.

His second marriage was no better. He was thirty-one this time and he opened his front door to an Avon lady and Mary Kay representative with brown doe-like eyes, wearing a two-piece mushroom coloured suit with a lace shirt and black and white polka dot high heel shoes. They were married two weeks later in Las Vegas. This marriage lasted nine years until he found out she was running around with the local real estate agent.

There was a third one. He was forty-two this time and he was seated on a plane headed to Rio, on his first mural painting assignment. This time, it was a twenty-nine-year-old air flight attendant in a cute little uniform, which showed off long, tanned legs and under a tilted navy cap, she had a winsome smile. Her platinum-coloured hair was tied back in a neat, tight ponytail. They were married four months later and divorced two years down the track. This last one tried to take him to the cleaners but he hired the best lawyer he could comfortably afford. After that, he gave up on the idea of marriage, preferring casual relationships. He still lived in hope of finding his one true love someday.

He looked around the main street of Brumby Flat which was now a hive of activity with reporters, police, university law students on a field trip, curious strangers driving through and nosy locals. He turned to go back home, to his 'on loan' farmhouse. He was not comfortable in crowds which is why he lived very inconspicuously in New York. There, he could be a nobody and blend in, or be that somebody if he needed to be.

Back at the Brumby Flat post office, Bridie was slowly getting on top of the situation she was dealing with. Thankfully, the inflatable raft was starting to shrink in size. She was still half-naked, only wearing her skinny jeans and had started to look around for her black T-shirt. She left the raft hissing away in the corner of the room and walked behind the high shop counter. She was sure she had thrown her top there but after glancing up and around, it was still missing. She couldn't really open the front door to parcel deliveries or locals without all her clothes on. That would certainly stir up all the gossips in town.

However, Bridie was used to being the talk of the town. It had been that way all her life. Bridie had come from a broken home and entered foster care at an early age. In her youth, she had been quite rebellious, often in trouble with foster parents, school teachers and on occasion, even the local police. She did not like rules, as a rule and if her foster parents seemed unreasonable about anything, she would not go home. She would sleepover on a friends' couch. One time, she walked through a farmers' paddock and took their tractor which still had the keys in the ignition for a hair-raising spin right through the middle of Brumby Flat. She was just twelve years old when it happened and she was sent to stay at another foster parent's home after that. She already smoked, she drank hard and hung out with the local lads before she had turned thirteen. She never finished high school, preferring to party long, hard and hang out with a rough crowd. She got expelled from school several times. When she turned eighteen, she left town for a couple of years but was drawn back to Brumby Flat like a magnet. She did not do much when she returned, just more of the same, drinking, smoking and hanging out with the bad boys until one day, she heard that the post office might be closing down forever. The old lady running it had decided to retire at ninety-two. Bridie saw it as a great opportunity to make a future for herself and improve her reputation in town. She took the business on and it worked for a short while, but then she started to have too much fun flirting with the men and boyfriends in town. Before too long, the rumour mill had a head start on her, so Bridie was forced to play catch up. In the end, she found comfort in the arms of a number of married men. The town believed she was a man-eater so she merely began to play the part and she played it very well.

Bridie was so preoccupied with her search for her missing T-shirt behind the front counter that she didn't hear the back door creak open. But she did hear a floorboard creak in the direction of the backroom and that got her immediate attention.

Thinking it was Phil Proctor returning, she half-smiled and shook her head, "Hey, cowboy, did you leave something behind, buddy? Have you seen my black tee? It seems to have vanished," she called out, putting her hands on her hips

"Well, come out. Don't be shy now. You weren't shy with me before."

There was no answer. She turned her back to the doorway and looked over the floor again. She assumed that she had imagined it. No one else was there with her.

When she finally turned around, her eyes widened in fear and her right arm automatically went up in defence. She managed to mouth the word 'no' but the first blow was swift and then, a series of blows rained down on her head, increasingly strong and vicious.

When it was all over and Bridie had fallen silent, her body slumped over the front counter. The figure put the bloody weapon into a plastic bag and retreated through the backdoor, latching it behind them with a gloved hand. Then, they slipped away undetected.

Chapter Five

It was like a warm Spring day in Brumby Flat. The blowflies were making a nuisance of themselves as Raquel Willaston walked determinedly to the local post office the next morning. She had to pay a couple of bills and do some banking. She studied the shop front curiously and rechecked her Swiss watch and her mobile phone. It was thirty-five past nine but there was no open sign out on the pavement or 'Open' sign on the front door. She thought it was odd but knowing Bridie's reputation around town, she was probably hungover or overslept with her new squeeze. She knocked on the shop door a couple of times but evidently, there was no action happening there yet.

She turned around and literally bumped into Senior Detective Phil Duncan. He was outfitted in a simple white shirt with a fine navy pinstripe and conservative grey trousers.

"Hey, Raquel, how are you?"

She tried to push past him but he stood firm, like a statue, in front of her. Blowflies swooped and darted around them in crisscross patterns.

"Bloody hell!" she exclaimed, "Oh, it's you. Well, what do you want? Haven't you deceived me enough already? I know what you're all about," She faced him, hands on hips.

He coughed nervously, "Well, look, I know we had a bad start. I want to make it up to you. I wanted to ask you out on a date tonight."

"A date? Are you for real, detective?"

He nodded his head, "I am serious. I am really sorry that I deceived you. I realise that it was wrong. I am just asking you to forgive me, if you can. And to let me set things right. Anyway, I finish work at half past five today. We can go out at six if you want. Up to you…but I am serious. I want to say sorry and take you out. Properly."

"Did you say tonight?"

"Yes. Tonight. A proper dining out experience. I'll take you to the pub. They say the foods really good. Just say yes and give me another chance. That's all I am asking."

She wasn't too keen on the idea. However, she could see he was trying. She reluctantly agreed by inclining her head.

He smiled slightly, "Wonderful. Thanks. I'll pick you up at six."

"Don't be late. Otherwise, you may upset me again," she called after him.

He kept on walking but waved his hand in the air as he retreated.

It was the final big moving day. Raquel was busy helping Bette and her shop volunteer Chris shift the last of the merchandise into the new shop. She took a coffee break after two hours of solid work and stood under the front veranda, enjoying the warm sunshine on her face, just for a moment. Since she had moved to Brumby Flat, there had not been one drop of rain.

Raquel took in an audible sharp intake of breath when she saw Phil Proctor in the distance, on the hillside at the far end of the main street. She knew it was him in an instant. She found it hard to believe that he was sixty-six years old, as he was so tanned, fit and looked majestic in his Driza-Bone, sitting perfectly poised on his borrowed black thoroughbred mare. He saw her too and tipped his brand new Akubra hat in her direction.

That was it. There were butterflies dancing and fluttering around in the pit of her stomach. She stood there a little bit taller on her tiptoes and gave him a little wave back.

Her friend Bette had noticed it first. She had introduced most of the who's who in town to Phil Proctor as soon as he arrived but she did notice Raquel was a bundle of nerves and her legs were jelly when she finally met him that morning and shook his very strong, outstretched hand. Strangely, Raquel could not even put four words together and she giggled far too much when Proctor said something he thought, of course, was funny, which, no one else did.

Bette walked out of the shop just then, dressed uncharacteristically casual in stretch blue jeans and a white starched linen shirt and took it all in. She saw Proctor riding away, up the hill.

"Oh dear god, girl," Bette shook her head, "What *is* going on with you two?"

"Wh-what do you mean?" Raquel replied, clearing her throat and hoping her cheeks were not flushed.

"You and Proctor of course. You have the hots for him, don't you?"

Raquel folded her arms, "Don't be ridiculous. He's far too old for me. And he is not my type at all."

Bette nodded her head, "Oh yes he is. Let's see…He's an artist. He's tall and he's American. You think he's quite the cowboy, doll."

Raquel could feel her cheeks getting hot and smiled, "Damn it, Bette. Okay. Okay. There's something about him that just…drives me crazy. Maybe it's his American accent. I don't know what it is about him, but he's definitely sexy."

Bette chuckled, "You've got a crush on the poor bloke."

Her new friend shrugged her shoulders and leaned against a veranda post.

"Maybe he likes you too, doll."

"I highly doubt it. I made an idiot of myself earlier."

Proctor had disappeared over the hill but then, a minute later, he reappeared. He was riding the black mare at a swift trot. He stopped her at the edge of the fence line.

Then Raquel saw him motion with his right arm. He made a wide arc with his arm, beckoning her to come over. Or so it looked like he was.

"Well, doll. Looks like you're up. Here's your chance to make an impression."

Raquel smiled back at her friend, "Yep, hope he's up to it. See you later, Bette…maybe."

She walked to her car, a Pontiac Firebird and drove up the dirt track on the hill. She had been told that Proctor's farmhouse lay at the end of the road.

She drove through the inviting open white gates of lot five Shelley Drive and parked in the centre of his gravel driveway. Before she was prepared to knock on his front door, she quickly glanced in the car mirror and fixed up her makeup. But not too much as she believed he liked natural-looking women.

She admired the farmhouse. It was an old fibreboard cottage painted white with big picture book windows, the frames of which were painted bright red. The roof was made of what they called ninety-nine-year-old iron.

She strolled up to the front door and before she could knock, she noticed a scrawled note pinned to it. It said in his scrawly writing "You'll find me in the stables."

She smiled, took the note down and slipped it into her shirt top pocket. It was a nice memento for her to keep. She heard him whispering to the black mare in the stables before she actually saw him. He turned at her footsteps echoing across the cement floor.

"This is a good note for a killer to find," she reached into her pocket and unravelled the piece of paper.

He smiled wryly back at her. That was the most un-giggly words he'd got out of her yet, which completely surprised him.

He took off his dusty Akubra hat and studied her with his intensely attractive blue eyes.

"Well, okay. Ma'am, I appreciate your concern about my health, safety and welfare. But I know how to look after myself," he drawled.

She felt a bit silly and went super-shy again. It was left to him to break the ice.

"I thought I'd invite you over for a coffee. Or tea if you would prefer. Maybe show you my rough sketches and plans for the town's goat mural. If you are interested, that is."

"Love to."

"Well, that's just great."

"She's a beauty."

"The mare? Yeah, she is. I'll just finish up in here. She needs a light rub down. The back door is open. Please, ma'am. Go inside and make yourself real comfortable."

She thought that was a great idea. She wanted to have a nosy around the cottage and pick up some ideas about Phil Proctor.

The country style kitchen with solid timber benches gave away no clues so she walked through to the lounge room, trying to get a sense of what kind of a man he was. Bette had said he had arrived at Adelaide airport with five full suitcases. The farmhouse had minimal furniture, but she did notice a handful of books on the timber coffee table. They were classic novels from the 1800s. She picked up one and studied the elegant binding and read the preface. Somewhere in the hallway, she heard a ticking grandfather clock. It made a pleasing melodic sound, reminding her of her great grandmother's home.

She returned the book to the coffee table when she saw a framed photograph on the sideboard. She studied it closely. It was in black and white of a young Phil Proctor smiling and posing in his high school football uniform, holding his helmet with the look of pride.

Suddenly, she felt like she was being watched. The hair on the back of her neck stood up. She glanced back, and through the corner of her eye, she was certain she had seen a flicker of movement.

"Hello? Is that you, Proctor?" she piped up, but seconds passed with no answer in return.

She started to slowly creep backwards, towards the kitchen doorway and she was certain she heard a footfall and some small rattling sound. A shadow suddenly passed through the hallway and Raquel didn't hold back. She screamed as hard as she could and raced into the kitchen. Something or rather someone started running down the narrow hallway and she clearly heard the heavy front door slam shut.

Proctor had heard her scream and ran in from the stables to her rescue. He had just removed his dusty Akubra and Driza-Bone. He removed his pocket knife from his Levi's and as soon as he got through the backdoor, he also grabbed a carving knife from the knife block in his other hand. He found Raquel wide-eyed and backed up against the kitchen sink.

"Are you okay?" he asked her in a sharp whisper.

She nodded, "There was someone in here. They went through the front door. No, no, don't go…Don't leave me alone."

Proctor juggled the knives into his right hand and touched her arm gently to reassure her. He then raced to the front door and looked out. If someone had been in his house, they were well and truly gone, escaping through the dense bushes and gumtrees in the side paddock.

When he returned to the kitchen, Raquel had relaxed and was leaning over his chopping board on wheels. He casually popped the big knife back into the knife block.

"Whoever it was. They're off and they're gone. Are you really okay?"

"Yes, yes. It just shook me up. It was creepy. They were in here, like, watching me. I felt it."

"Umm. You are thinking the killer of that guy was in here? With you?"

She rolled her shoulders which were feeling a bit tight, "I am not too sure. It crossed my mind but could be local kids too. Or some thief. Bette, my friend, reckons we've got lots of strangers hanging around town since the murder."

Proctor nodded his head in agreement, his eyes squinting as he looked out the back door with the sun high and full in the cloudless sky. She forgot how tall he was, so she stood up straight to quietly admire his physique.

"Yes, ma'am. I know few people here, but you would."

"I have only lived here for three months."

"Sorry honey, but what's your name again?"

She blushed, "You're teasing me. But my name's Raquel Willaston."

"I'm Proctor, Phil Proctor."

"I know. I think we all know who you are."

"Do you prefer me to call you Raquel or is Willow okay?" he smirked.

"Raquel is fine."

Proctor suddenly picked her up like a Barbie doll in his muscular arms and sat her down on the edge of his kitchen table. She took a big gasp of breath and felt a bit dizzy. He was certainly strong and definitely, he was a man's man.

"Look here, young lady," he said in his gruff whisper of a voice, half leaning against her and the table edge, "I have seen it all. I know what this little old town is like. It might be Australia, but a small town is exactly what it is, wherever it is. A hot den of dirty little secrets. For sure, this town is hot, dry and dusty. I reckon there's a lot of mean and frustrated people living around us, but you can trust me. Do you trust me, Raquel?"

His close proximity to her being, made her feel hot, steamy and giddy. She pressed into him slightly more, "Yeah, I get that from you," she replied, trying to appear unruffled.

He nodded his head, his weathered but handsome face inching that bit closer to her own pretty, unblemished one, "I have been watching some folks around here. I can't discuss what I've seen with you. I can't tell you right now what I already know. What I have seen. If I say anything at all, well, it might be dangerous. To us both, if you are understanding what I am saying."

She nodded enthusiastically. She was intrigued that he had ideas about the killer's identity already.

He smirked, "I don't think the killer just came to pay me a visit now. But from now on, I'm gonna keep my doors locked. And so should you, girlie."

His face came even closer and his breath came hot and heavy against her left cheek.

"Proctor," she said, finding her voice trembling just a little, "Honestly, I am scared. I moved here with...I mean, I moved here for a tree change and I've certainly got it. The region's in the grip of a massive drought. The people here are really, really...different. There's a, a murderer running around loose. And...any one of us could be the next to go. That's what Bette in Raindrops says."

"Well, I care about you, Raquel. I would not let anything happen to you. I fancy your nifty little car too," he quipped light-heartedly, flashing his best wry smile.

At that, he took her face gently in both his broad, tanned hands and kissed her. It only lasted a couple of seconds or so, but it was firm, warm, sweet and the sensation of it lingered with her long after the kiss was over and his presence was gone. It was like the spark to a firecracker, a flicker to a flame. The kiss took her breath away and her legs were jelly. He was well experienced with women. She had no doubt about it now. It was all in that one bold kiss.

"Oh god, I am so confused," she shook her head, and a small tear made its lonely way down her left cheek.

"Sweetheart, what have you got to be confused about?" he said softly.

"I think this is way too fast. You were going to show me the mural. That's what you said."

She jumped off the kitchen table, slipped under his strong, outstretched arms and backed away, towards the back door.

"I have to go now. Bye."

Proctor liked her. She was not outgoing like the bird Bridie Browne was. This one was shy, a bit reserved and downright awkward. He said nothing more and let her go her own way. He sat down at the kitchen table and thought about kissing her soft, full lips for a long while after.

Chapter Six

Raquel had returned to the post office soon after seeing Proctor. There was still no open sign out anywhere, and still no answer to her loud and persistent knocking. The blowflies seemed to be multiplying and buzzing madly around her face. She gave up and returned to the shop to see how Bette and Chris were going.

Bette was now wearing a stylish outfit of cream stretch jeans with a V-neck floral top. She had a pair of nineteen-seventies platform shoes on which gave her a little extra height. Chris was in his usual army fatigues and Anabella had just arrived to lend a daintily gloved hand. But Raquel wondered how useful she would be, as she was dressed in a pink pastel floral dress with a pleated full skirt. She had pale pink gloves on this time and carried a wicker basket handbag on her right arm. A wide-brimmed straw hat with matching pink scarf finished off her outfit. Because she was hot with all her nylon and lace petticoats underneath, she was fanning her face with a small Chinese fan She looked very Audrey Hepburn-like today, Raquel thought to herself.

"Hey, the shop's looking really amazing now. I leave for three seconds and it's all changed again," Raquel could see how much more progress had been made.

Snow skis, tarpaulins, water skis, umbrellas, raincoats and gumboots were arranged in neat rows, no doubt aided by Chris. There was still a couple of things to sort out, but for the most part, the Raindrops Shop was ready to impress.

"Yes, I'm very pleased with it," Bette announced in her raspy voice.

At this point, Senior Detective Duncan walked in, his eyeglasses rims twinkling in the strong sunlight.

Raquel gasped and looked at her watch. He was early by a good hour.

"Well. Are you trying hard to impress me or something?" she said sarcastically.

Duncan smirked, "Something. No. Actually, I'm still struggling a bit. I came by for another latte. Need it today."

"Is it about the murder? Do you know who the stranger is?" Anabella piped up, her eyes widened in excitement.

"Who he was," he corrected her, then added, "I can't talk about the case. But since I am here, I did want to ask if anything else unusual happened a few days ago."

There was a brief silence.

"Well. It's the second day the post office has been unfortunately closed," Raquel said with a casual shrug of her shoulders and a roll of her hazel eyes.

Bette's eyes glazed over and she turned her attention to Chris, "Hey. Have you seen Bridie around, Chris?"

He shook his head, "I've been twice to the post office the last two days, exactly at Thirteen hundred hours, eight minutes and fifteen seconds and there's been no answer to my hard knocking. No sign out either. The curtains have been closed too."

"Detective Duncan, that's highly unusual. Even for our Bridie," Bette said.

"And I have to say, also, the blowflies are pretty bad on that side of…"

Raquel's voice faded away as all five of them took a few seconds to swap concerned looks at each other. Senior Detective Duncan was the first to sprint into action, with Chris charging up the rear, probably like he used to do in the army reserve. The ladies trotted briskly after them, Anabella running on tiptoes because of her high heels and her basketweave bag still hanging high on her right wrist. With her other gloved hand, she was struggling to keep her straw hat in position.

Duncan knocked loudly on the post office front door and cried out Bridie's name. There was no answer from within. Chris knocked loudly after him and yelled out in his best command voice. But still, no answer came from within.

"Is there a back door?"

Chris nodded, "I'll check it out."

Less than thirty seconds later, he returned, "It's locked, sir."

"Has anyone else got a key?"

"No, not as far as I know. Bridie is the only employee and works the post office alone," Bette said, her voice starting to tremble.

Duncan looked at Chris, "How hard can it be? We could knock the bloody door down."

"I've got a crowbar in my jeep."

Duncan nodded, "Definitely a better idea."

He looked at Anabella who was pressing into his back. She looked ready to fly into the post office and feed her curiosity.

"Now ladies, please stay here, stay calm and above all else, stay outside."

The crowbar proved successful enough, in the end, to pry open the front door and Duncan and Chris entered the post office together. There was a foul, rotting stench in the dusty air which explained the swarming blowflies.

Duncan visibly flinched when he saw what was left of Bridie draped over the high timber counter. She was completely topless and he assumed she could be easily naked behind the counter. Her skull was bashed in, also her left shoulder blade was shattered, with congealed blood in her curly hair and streaming down to a dry burgundy coloured puddle on the floor. Bits of splintered bone, facial and brain tissue fanned out all over the counter and nearby walls. Chris gulped at the unpleasant murder scene and backed out of the front door. The putrid smell of rotting flesh had hit him particularly hard.

His face was ash white when he got outside and Bette, Raquel and Anabella knew instantly the news was not good indeed.

Duncan whipped his mobile phone out of his top shirt pocket and quickly dialled a number.

"Longmeil. Yeah, it's me. We've got another dead body in town. At the local post office. Better call it in. I'll wait here for you."

****

"Well. It's the big dead dry," Raquel half-whispered the words as she sat in Bette and Sandy's swinging egg chair on their back porch.

Bette leaned forward under her wicker and canvas-covered cabana, perching her prescription aviators on the bridge of her nose. She had her sleek bobbed hair peeking out under a floppy hat, along with her vivid blue jay peepers. She was dressed in her itsy-bitsy barely enough room for a polka dot bikini. An impressive minuscule garment for a woman in her late thirties.

"What was that, doll? What did you say?"

Raquel had been invited over to their impressive three-storey home on the only hill around, on the edge of town to enjoy a quiet three-course dinner, over a chilled bottle of French champagne and a bottle of Grange from their wine cellar. She was invited over as Senior Detective Duncan had to postpone their planned second date, due to the second murder.

"Sorry. I was just thinking aloud…very dry and dusty out here. These are very unsettling times. I thought this was going to be a quiet place to live in."

Bette nodded, "Yes, terrible. What an awful business. Poor Bridie. I didn't like her personally, as you well know. But no one deserves to die the horrible way that she did."

"I don't want to think about it. Her poor family, how they must be feeling tonight."

"Naw. Our poor Bridie had no family. That's why she was a wild child type. She lived with a local family here though, but I heard they had real problems with her. She didn't take orders from anyone. She did whatever she wanted to do. Always in some kind of trouble, she was."

Raquel raised an eyebrow at this revelation, "Oh my god. Really? How sad."

"Never mind, doll. Here's some more champagne. Are you putting on your swimmers?"

"I don't know. I can hear all these noises around us. I wonder where it's coming from."

Bette sniffed and gestured with her thumb up, "Ah. It's just all my paying guests upstairs."

"Oh sorry. You have other guests?"

"Well, there was no accommodation in town, and all of our out of towners asked me about rooms to rent. I thought, what the hell. So we've let out five rooms upstairs to some reporters and the two detectives. The uni law students are bunked in one room together too. They seem happy enough. I'm running it like a B&B, without the second 'B' in it. I don't have time to make the 'B' for breakfast part."

"So, just one 'B'. Yeah, I get that."

"The spa's nice and relaxing. It's a brand-new swim spa."

Raquel shook her head, "I can't. I had a worrying experience at Proctor's house the other day. I don't think I can totally relax here, or anywhere else."

Bette removed her aviators in a sweeping gesture, concerned for her friend and also realised that the sun had finally gone down and she didn't need them anymore, "Oh dear. What on earth happened up there? Do you want to talk about it, doll?"

"It's okay. It wasn't anything Proctor did or said. He told me to go inside his house and wait for him. But someone was like hiding in there. I could feel someone was watching me. They ran out the front door. I didn't see who it was. I've been stressed out ever since. I keep thinking was it the killer?"

"Doll, more reason for you to try to unwind."

"I don't know how you do it, Bette. You look fantastic and you're so laid back tonight."

"Well, I am now making money, hand over fist. As you know, this drought was really affecting my business, but the murder of that stranger, well. I know I shouldn't be saying this, but it's been a blessing in disguise."

"Yeah, you are very busy with coffees and now you're letting out your rooms."

"And don't forget someone responsible in town has to look after all our letters and parcels. I might have to learn to manage that side as well." She lifted her full glass and tapped Raquel's soundly.

"Oh yes. You're right. We still need a working post office."

"Lucky for us Bridie was not sorting the mail when she, unfortunately…dropped off her perch," she glanced down at her watch, "Well. Time for dinner, I think. I've cooked my famous Italian meatballs and spaghetti for mains."

She got off her cabana and cupped her hands around her lips, yelling out at the top of her raspy voice, "PANDY MANDY SANDY! DINNER!"

"Who are you calling?"

Bette reclined back again, adjusting her very tiny bikini top, "Pandora, our cat. And my Sandy of course. I think he's putting the floodlights on our tennis court. Should be back in a minute or so."

"Wow, I didn't know you guys had a tennis court too."

"It's just a half court tennis court, doll."

The cat suddenly appeared out from the shadows, but it made Raquel jump in fright and spill her glass of champagne over her brand-new leopard print skirt. It was a Russian Blue with just one blue eye, a crooked tail and half her left ear missing. She wasn't a particularly pretty cat. And her answering meow was really a low snarling sound.

"Hey, my Pandy-Mandy," Bette cooed over her much-adored fur baby, "Poor darling girl. She's been in the wars since we moved here two years ago. I think she's used up eight of her nine lives. She's been run over by a semi. Bitten by a brown snake. Been attacked by the corgi next door and locked in a neighbour's shed for a week. And she was accidentally shot on the local rifle range. Then just last week, she jumped on a window sill upstairs. The window was wide open and she fell three stories."

"Shit. That's some CV for a cat."

Sandy suddenly appeared out of the shadows, but he didn't scare Raquel quite as much as their cat had.

"Hey, Raquel, how are you?" He said brightly, walking briskly past in his tropical print boardshorts and a thick mat of brown curly chest hair on show. He wore it all like a badge of honour. He was Bette's long tall glass of lemonade.

"Good, thanks."

"Bette, babe, do you want me to get the sauna going for you guys?"

"No dear. All good. Not going in the swim spa tonight."

"Bette," Raquel put on her serious tone of voice.

"Yes doll?"

"You can't run the whole town by yourself. I was thinking…I could be another volunteer for your shop. I think you could use my help."

"That's wonderful but what about your job?"

Her friend shrugged her shoulders, "All good. I can work around work. I don't work every day. I'm owed flexidays, annual leave and also have a volunteer's day off, I think. My boss is very laid back."

"Oh good. I think I have to do a quick lesson or two in the mail. Now before dinner, would you like Sandy to make you up a special cocktail? He's a whiz at that sort of thing."

Suddenly, they heard loud male voices echoing from upstairs.

Bette leaned forward again in her cabana and whispered just loud enough for Raquel only to hear her, "We have to be very careful about what we say. The newspaper reporters are on the second floor and they're always listening out for a story. I have to be quiet when I walk past their room. They're sharing the floor with the criminal law students who are researching for their studies. Or something like that. On the very top floor, your Detective friend and his Detective mate are trying to keep wraps on everything, I think. You don't hear a peep out of them at all."

She then let out a loud burp, "Excuse me."

Raquel widened her eyes, "Oh my god. I think you're a little bit drunk. Never seen you drunk before."

Bette giggled, "Yes, well, the secret's out. I've had two glasses of this yummy champagne and at least two screwdrivers before you came. But I'm okay. I am still thinking. I'm as sharp as a tack, doll."

"I have no doubt. What's for dinner again?"

Chapter Seven

Senior Detective Phillip Duncan really enjoyed the investigative aspect of his police work, but one thing he was not comfortable with was relaying bad news to families. He found this a particularly hard thing to do and it always made him think of his missing parents all those years ago. He secretly dreaded the day when he might learn of their fate too.

It had taken six long days to find the information needed to identify the dead stranger at the Brumby Flat silos. The dead stranger had carried no identification on him when he came to town. The backpack he was seen carrying had conveniently disappeared into thin air. Now Duncan had to approach what was left of the man's family who just happened to live in the town. But Detective Duncan knew the dead man's reappearance here was not a strange coincidence. Something had brought him back to confront his fears.

He came up to the low white picket fence with peeling paint and opened the small gate. He cautiously knocked on the front door of the gentleman's bungalow which had lost its glamorous grandeur a long time ago. He heard slow footsteps echoing down the hallway and the door finally swung open. Behind the broken screen door, an elderly lady peered out at him. She was hunched over a little, so she had to tilt her head up in order to view his face.

"Hello. Who are you?"

"I'm Senior Detective Duncan. From Adelaide."

He lifted up his badge and ID for her to see, "May I please come inside and talk to you."

Her grey head nodded a little as she unlatched the screen door.

He walked into the hallway which was full of antiques and dusty animal trophies. She half walked, half shuffled ahead of him, taking him to the front lounge room, which was filled with much the same, except for the addition of an old three-seater club lounge. She balanced her reading glasses on the tip of her nose to return to her knitting. She was dressed in a faded floral housecoat and wore insanely smiling unicorn silver glitter slippers on her feet. He guessed it was a recent purchase or more than likely, a gift.

"Mrs Elaine Burford?" he asked, as he sat down on the other end of the couch.

"Yes, that's my name," she said in a soft elderly tone of voice. She was eighty-eight, if she was a day, "I was expecting Meals on Wheels, not you."

"I have some news about your son Christopher."

She frowned, stopped her knitting and lay it down on her wide lap. She studied the detective more closely, taking in his sombre demeanour and conservative grey pinstripe suit.

"Oh stop it. He's been dead for over thirty years. You must know that."

Duncan pushed his glasses back as they had slipped down his nose, "And your husband's no longer with us?"

She visibly frowned again, "Yes, my poor Glen passed away. December four last year."

"Has your son been here to see you?"

"Pardon me?"

"That's my real question to you. Have you seen him recently?"

"Are you mad? He's dead. My son is very much dead, detective."

She frowned and returned to her knitting.

"Why are you really here, detective? What do you want?"

"I don't know how to tell you this, Mrs Burford but…your son Christopher, he was alive. He was alive and breathing. But he was killed earlier this week. His body was found at the base of the silos. I am very sorry to inform you."

Mrs Burford rested her knitting again in her lap and shook her head, "No. What rubbish. That's impossible. We buried him in the ground over thirty years ago. We had his funeral, for God's sake."

"I don't know who's buried in the cemetery but it's definitely not your son. He's been alive. He was alive until six days ago."

"You're lying. Why are you lying to me?"

"No, I'm not. Pardon the pun, but I'm deadly serious."

Silence descended. Mrs Burford took off her reading glasses and started to cry. She softly sobbed for a good minute and then wiped her teary eyes with her hands.

"My Christopher, he was alive?"

Duncan nodded, "Yes, he was. He may have returned here, to Brumby Flat to see you."

"Where the hell's he been? All these years? Why did he come back now?"

"From what we know so far, he's been living along the New South Wales coast."

She had gone from sad to angry at the turn of a phrase.

"Why? Why do that to your own mother? I loved my son. I always wanted to protect him. He was all we had."

"I have no doubt that you did your best."

She went quiet for a long minute and Duncan said nothing.

"But why was he hiding? Why hide from us, his loving parents? We thought he died years ago. It weakened my poor Glen's heart, I'm sure of it. We were never the same after it happened."

Duncan leaned forward on the edge of the couch, "Which brings me to ask you. Mrs Burford. What exactly happened thirty-two years ago? Is there a reason your son Christopher would have involved himself in some sort of deception? Why did he have to leave town in a hurry? Was he in some sort of trouble? Can you remember anything?"

She was thinking very hard but he could see she was lost in her thoughts.

"I'm sorry detective. It was such a long time ago. We were told that he died in a car crash. His car overturned and rolled on Old Emu Road. It happened about two in the morning. We were asked to come down and identify him. We couldn't see his face properly, due to his injuries. He was so badly burnt."

"So it looked like it might have been Christopher."

"Yes. That's right. The clothes were Christopher's."

Detective Duncan lightly coughed to clear his throat, "I think this is a big cover-up. Basically, we need to know *who* was buried in Christopher's place thirty-two years ago. We need your permission to exhume the gravesite. I can approach a magistrate to get it, but I'm asking you. I would prefer to have your permission."

Mrs Burford sighed heavily and cupped her right hand over her mouth.

"I'm not sure…if we should. You don't want to disrespect the dead, you know."

"I understand your concern, Mrs Burford. I don't like the thought of doing it either but we need to know why your son had to leave town all those years ago. Who died to cover his tracks? That is a big question which deserves an answer. You're his mother. You have the right to know."

"Yes, of course."

"I would question the coroner involved, but sadly he's gone. He died some years ago."

"I guess you are right. If my Christopher is dead now, who did we bury? Who did we have a service for?"

"Exactly. Let's find out, Mrs Burford."

She started to sob again, this time it lasted over five minutes and Detective Duncan understood how hard this was for her.

For the next hour and a half, Detective Duncan spent the time trying to reassure Mrs Burford, at times console her and finally secure her signature on the papers for the exhumation. He was mentally drained, but he still had more work to do. There was still the murder of Bridie Browne to investigate.

****

Raquel was driving back to Brumby Flat when a call came through on her Bluetooth.

"Hey, honey, how are you?"

It was her son Steve. He slept during the day and worked at night, so they rarely talked anymore.

"Good, Raquel. Where are you now?"

"Driving home from work."

He laughed, "You're never at work."

"Because I am so good and quick at my job, I can afford to spend so much more time away from it. One day, you might achieve this level of perfection too."

"Yeah, right. Anyway, I'm coming home tonight."

"No, Steve, please stay at Nan's place. There's been another murder up here."

"You're kidding."

"It's true. Google it. This time, the Post Mistress was bashed to death. I'd feel a lot better if you stayed away. It's not safe with a murderer running around."

"What about you?"

"Don't worry. I'll keep my windows and doors closed. And I'll keep a weapon at the front door."

"You got a gun? Really?" he exclaimed.

"No. That mural painter guy dropped off a horsewhip for me."

"Hmm. Is that for him?"

"You're so funny. Got to go now. I am doing my first volunteer gig at the Raindrops Shop," she steered the car to a stop outside their home in the main street.

"Okay, mother dear. Be careful. And good luck with your volunteering."

"Thanks. Love you, honey."

Bette had told her that she was shift sharing with Anabella Williams today. Raquel was happy about that as she had been the first volunteer and knew the ropes.

Anabella was already in the shop, flittering around the shop counter and tables full of merchandise with a feather duster which had seen better days. She was softly humming to herself. She had already had a very busy morning and yet still managed to look an immaculate picture of vintage style. She was wearing a pale blue V-neck dress with short sleeves and a full pleated skirt. Her silver-grey hair was trussed up in a sleek ponytail with a butter-coloured pillbox hat. She had been wearing tan gloves but had delicately removed them so she could clean up. Her handbag carefully hidden under the counter was barrel-shaped with a timber and leather trim. She had put out ten umbrellas and a pair of snow skis which featured the same blue hue as in her dress.

Before she came to the shop that morning, she had even finished baking a couple of tray loads of her peach and mango cupcakes. One tray load was a special order while the second batch was for the Raindrops Shop. Since the murders, Brumby Flat's population had virtually doubled in size overnight. Strangers were in and out of the shop most of the day, grabbing take away coffees and Anabella's homemade baked goods. The crowd-pleasing favourite was her peach and mango cupcakes.

Unfortunately, the orders got completely mixed up that morning. Anabella had been too busy doing her cat's eye makeup in her Hollywood style bathroom when the gentleman appeared to take his special order away.

"Your tray is on the left, on the bench," she yelled out to the gentleman standing in the kitchen.

He didn't know his left from his right and accidentally picked up the wrong tray. It was actually crucial for her not to mix up these batches of cupcakes for her own special reasons.

In the meantime, the wrong batch of cupcakes was safely under glass, sitting on a shiny silver cake stand, and Raquel had already noticed them.

"Hi, Anabella. Wow. They look lovely."

She smiled sweetly and nodded, "They're my very special peach and mango cupcakes. My husband loves them, you know."

Raquel didn't know what to say so she said nothing in response. She picked up a broom in the corner and proactively started to sweep the front veranda. It was another warm but dusty day, with a bit of wind whipping up the dirt at street level. She preferred to be outside anyway, taking in the surroundings and scanning the landscape for Phil Proctor. She was hoping to have another encounter with him but at the same time, she felt conflicted as well. The other Phil had asked her out again and she had said yes.

She swept for five minutes, but there was no sign of Proctor on his black mare. So she returned inside as the law students jostled in, all blurry-eyed from a night on the books and beer to get their morning coffee fix. It was their way of dealing with the isolation, the drought and the whiff of murder around them, by pretending they were ordering and sipping their soy lattes and dirty chai's in a city main street café. They lined up at the counter and Anabella took their orders with pencil and paper pad. She was usually not good with technology but she had mastered the coffee machine. No one wanted a cupcake, but Raquel was circling the glass dome with its glittering silver tray, thinking about it. But she was denied the opportunity with the confident and breezy arrival of local Lord Mayor Mrs Maggie Jarvis.

Mrs Jarvis was fifty-ish and always had a grumpy expression on her ashen face as if twenty years of local council in various modes of servitude had been a terrific burden to her. Her broad, flat face was framed by a short, very tight perm. She was an icy pair of eyes, a ski slope nose and a thin pair of lips hovering over her nineteen-eighties red power suit. She wore sensible low plain brown leather shoes with gold buckles and always carried a clipboard in her right hand, to enhance her image of being highly efficient. She carried her purse and her orange lippy in her skirt hip pocket. Never a handbag.

"Hello, Mrs Williams," she roared, as her voice had no lower range whatsoever. Over time, she had grown quite accustomed to shouting above disruptive members of council.

"Thought I'd come by and support the Raindrops Shop today."

"Mayor Maggie Jarvis, this is Raquel. She just moved into Brumby Flat."

Raquel had to look up and strain her neck as Mrs Jarvis was quite tall and Amazon-like in build. Standing at around five foot ten, she cut an intimidating figure as well.

"Excellent. Brilliant. We need new blood around here. And what do you do, Raquel?"

"IT stuff. I am indispensable to my boss. I can walk in whenever I like, spend a short time there and it's all done. I have a lot of downtime, which is good."

Raquel felt obliged to keep it simple.

Mrs Jarvis nodded, "Well. Apart from being on Council, I am…"

Raquel lost interest after twenty-nine lines of description, punctuated with a lot of big wordy words she had not heard spoken before. In fact, she had suddenly acquired a headache, along with the crick in her neck.

Thankfully, Mrs Jarvis finished her long, loud and rambling account of her own self-importance to her local constituent and turned her full attention to the cupcakes.

"Did you cook these, Mrs Williams? They look positively grand, my dear."

Anabella nodded enthusiastically.

"They're my peach and mango cupcakes. Excuse me, I'll be back shortly."

Anabella dashed out in the midst of her coffee orders.

"I'll take all the cupcakes, dear," Mrs Jarvis said in her booming voice to Raquel.

Raquel found several paper bags under the counter and started filling them with the unusual smelling cupcakes. Perhaps they were more mango than peach, she thought to herself. She gave them to Mrs Jarvis in a large paper carry bag.

"They're three dollars each so that will be thirty-six dollars."

Mrs Jarvis waved a fifty dollar note in her face and said, "Keep the change. Put it in as my donation to the shop, to the community. Terrible hearing about all the murders in town."

"How very generous of you. Bette and the community will be pleased."

"I know. I like to be spontaneous, you know."

"Yes, I get that about you. Definitely."

Mrs Jarvis sniffed loudly and started briskly walking to the front door, announcing behind her, "Lovely to meet you. I am dying to get these cups of cake deliciousness home for hubby and myself to try. We'll have them with our afternoon Devonshire tea on my pink roses Royal Doulton tea set."

"Nice, nice," Raquel replied, flashing a tight-lipped smile.

In a second, Mrs Jarvis was gone and halfway down the main street already, on her way to her next community project.

Anabella returned immediately after Mrs Jarvis had left. It got Raquel thinking that maybe those two had an uncomfortable history.

Apart from the appearance of the law students and Mayor Mrs Maggie Jarvis, it proved to be a quiet day in the shop. There was a retired couple driving through in their insanely big, petrol-guzzling RV who stopped for a coffee break and bought the most expensive umbrella in the shop. They made a big deal about driving through the 'murder town'.

The local town drunk turned up later and he staggered around the merchandise tables like a seasoned Olympic ice-skater, with Anabella anxiously following behind him. He took an immediate dislike to Raquel.

At one point, he waved his crooked index finger in her face, and she could smell the whiskey on his breath.

"Who the fuck do you think you are, madam? You strut into town, like you friggin' own the place," he shouted, swaying on his feet, "Well, you bloody don't. You own shit and you know shit too."

Anabella steered him towards the door, "Now Jack, you shouldn't talk to the nice lady like that. She's just new here."

"I don't like her look," he growled.

"You don't have to like everyone in town."

"Hey, can I bum a fag off you?"

Anabella cringed and replied curtly, "I do not smoke. Oh look, I think the hotel's open now."

He staggered out the door, mumbling something.

After he was out, Anabella locked the door for a couple of minutes. She started to put on her hat and gloves, checking her vintage perfect reflection in the shop mirror.

"I hope you enjoyed your first day here," she said, patting a wisp of grey stray hair off her pale, heavily powdered face.

Raquel nodded, "So much fun. Anyway, got a hot date tonight. See you later."

Chapter Eight

Raquel arrived at the local pub which was very aptly named the Spur and Fetlock Hotel. Senior Detective Duncan had texted her ten minutes earlier, asking to just meet him inside. There were three external doors and two were locked so she eventually made it through the third one. Watching her enter the hotel, for Detective Duncan, it was a touch of Deja vu.

She had poured herself into a simple black V-neck dress with a leopard wrap draped across her shoulders. Leopard print flats and a knockoff black Prada handbag from Thailand completed her outfit. Her blond hair was loose and just sprayed over her shoulders. She looked directly at him, a blank look that he couldn't read.

She walked slowly up to him and he rose from the table like a gentleman. There wasn't much light in the hotel dining room. The carpet needed replacing, the walls needed painting, the timber ceiling was far too dark and the table linen covered the cheapness of the chipboard tables. The chairs were cheap plastic ones with tie on beige chair cushions.

There were quite a few locals gathered at surrounding tables, watching the lone country and western singer quickly setting up in a dark corner of the dining room to play a set for them. She was pretty and petite, wearing a pair of torn jeans, a fringed leather jacket over a plain V-neck tee and an Akubra hat way too big for her which half-covered her pretty eyes. She briefly wrestled with her guitar and then started to sing a well-known bush ballad in a high shrill pitch. She had a pleasant enough voice and a captive, appreciative audience.

Like their first meeting in the city, Duncan had stood up and shook her outstretched hand. The local crowd around them grumbled because they were standing in their way, so they sat down together very quickly. Raquel noticed how brilliant blue his eyes were behind his glasses again, but she still didn't like his near baldness. He was conservatively dressed in a brown pinstripe suit with a plain white shirt, no tie. They had to make a conscious effort to talk a little bit louder, over the singing.

He smiled and greeted her in his deep, strong voice, "Hello, Raquel. You look very beautiful tonight."

She felt her cheeks flush a rosy pink, "Don't try to flatter me. I still remember our date number one."

"I wish you would put it to bed. I did not think we would meet again. But we have. I am prepared to make amends. I shouldn't have lied to you."

"Bloody hell. You're right about that."

"Look, I do like you. I think because of my unusual…upbringing, I think I can't commit myself to any sort of relationship. Even friendship is hard for me. My childhood was a bit messy and complicated."

Raquel sighed heavily. She picked up the menu and started to scan it. Senior Detective Duncan decided to do the same and try to talk to her later, after they had ordered dinner.

"I think I'll order the battered fish and chips. Seeing I missed out on seafood last time."

Duncan rolled his eyes and sat far back in his chair, "Oh my god. Here we go again. We don't have to have dinner. Especially if you want to be difficult."

"Yeah, well. Let's not bother then," she snapped back.

A local tapped her on the shoulder and hushed her, indicating to the singer who had just launched into her second song.

"Don't you dare hush me," she responded sharply.

She turned to Duncan, "They shushed me. Do something about it?"

"Hey, I'm a detective, not your private peacekeeper."

"You're telling me."

"Fine. I've had a tough bloody day anyway. I don't need this attitude from you."

More locals grumbled at all the noise the pair of them were making.

Duncan snapped his menu shut and got up. She did the same and followed him. The locals looked relieved and continued to enjoy the singer's performance.

They both stomped out into the cool of the early evening. They turned around and faced each other, point-blank.

"It was never going to work between us."

She nodded and said disdainfully, "No. I really do dislike you, quite a lot."

He smirked again, "You frustrate me greatly."

"I have an attitude, have I?"

They kept staring at each other, but Duncan eventually broke the spell by taking a bold step forward and planting a firm kiss on her surprised lips. He had grabbed the small of her back and held her tight against him. She tried to push him away for half a second but then got right into it. Their tongues met and twirled. It was a thrilling, hot type of kiss. When he withdrew his lips, it left her wanting more.

"Your place or mine?" he asked her, virtually holding her up like a doll.

"Sex at my place," she snapped, but not as coldly as she had before.

"Fine. Good idea."

He let her go. She half staggered to her car, her head cloudy with decisions and overwhelmed with thoughts. She drove back home, behind Duncan's white station wagon.

At the front door, she fumbled with her huge set of keys which included keys from her last two houses. Duncan stood behind her real close, his fingers gently running up her skirt but with some discretion. A few people were walking their dogs up and down the main street. His breath came hot on the nape of her bare neck as he had swept her hair over one shoulder. She was bitten by a mosquito in the same spot but she did not really care about that.

Finally, the front door was flung wide open and Duncan half lifted her through the door. He slammed the door shut expertly with his foot. He had her cotton knickers down in a split second and her black satin bra flying off across the room the next.

"Gosh, you're fast," she exclaimed, gasping for breath as he nuzzled his face between her pendulum breasts.

"I want you now. You annoying little tart," he said in a low, deep voice which excited her and sent shivers up her spine. He looked and acted so conservatively, that his sudden burst of unbridled passion had caught her by complete surprise. She tore his shirt and he accidentally tore her dress sleeve as they abandoned all their clothing, threw off their expensive shoes and fell onto her four-poster queen bed in a sexual funk.

As they enjoyed trying several positions, Duncan proved to be an attentive lover. He took time to kiss her lips, her elbow, the base of her neck, the slight curve of her belly and her inner thighs. He found all her erogenous zones. He teased her nipples and she was impressed by his bigger than average cock. She let out an excited squeal when she saw him in his full naked glory.

After two hours, they lay back on her bed quite exhausted. They started to talk openly and to finally get to know each other. Senior Detective Duncan told her about his unconventional upbringing and Raquel told him about her failed circus performer career.

"Really?"

He was interested right away.

She showed him a long white scar on her left knee, "See this? I was on the highflying trapeze and I missed my cue. I fell straight down into the safety net but I bounced off the side of it. Cut my knee open, and that was the end of my career. Bingo Bango, it was all over."

"You must've been very flexible."

"I still am. I can do the splits, you know. And I can pull my legs right over my head. I can do a bridge and cartwheels."

Duncan smirked, "I'd like to see all that. Show me."

They proceeded to enjoy another two hours of particularly hot and athletic sex.

"Wow, that was unreal. What a talent."

Raquel pulled the sheet up around her, smiling at him, "Yeah, it wasn't too bad. Well, I guess that was it."

Duncan arched an eyebrow and made a sweeping gesture to put his glasses back on and then lay back down, "Okay. What do you mean by that?"

"Well, you know. That was a bit of fun."

"So, Raquel. Are you…looking for a relationship or just a good time?"

He peered at her through his glasses, his bright blue eyes dancing behind them.

She shrugged her shoulders, "Look, I don't want to upset you, Phil. But I'm not sure. I don't know what to do right this minute."

"Let's cuddle for a bit then."

She allowed him to put his right arm around her and she nestled into his warm, heaving chest. She was pleasantly surprised to find he was quite warm, even his hands were now hot to touch.

"Phil, I guess when these murders are resolved, everything goes back to how it was."

"Yeah, Brumby Flat is a normal small town again," he whispered and kissed the top of her head, with great gentleness and tenderness.

"No. I mean us. You go back to Adelaide. I will stay here."

He was quiet for a long minute.

"Ah okay. I get it. You think I go to bed with every woman I meet on that dating app."

"Well? Don't you? Haven't you?"

He frowned at her, removed his arm and general warmness. He got up lightning fast. He stood side on so she managed another quick glance at his impressive half erection.

"I said...I like you. Never mind. Guess I'll go now. Thanks and I hope you're less angry with me."

"See you around," she gave him a little awkward wave.

"Yeah. Sure. See you around."

He clicked his tongue in the weird way that he did.

He quickly pulled up his trousers, wrestled with his torn white shirt and picking up his shoes and jacket, he slipped quietly away.

Raquel heard her front door slam a few seconds later and she had time alone to rethink what she had said to him. She leaned forward in the bed with her knees up and put her flushed face in her hands.

"Oh my god. What the fuck have I done?" she exclaimed.

****

The next morning, Raquel went to her work for a couple of hours and noticed her boss was back from the sunny Gold Coast. She was aware of his presence in the office because of his hay fever but as usual, he kept a low profile and tiptoed past her door. As long as she did her work, he was happy enough with her efforts. He still didn't understand her mood swings and it was best to avoid her altogether. Whenever she yelled out his name, usually the first sign of trouble, he would run out the back door.

"I'm off now," she yelled out into the foyer but as usual there came no answer.

As soon as she turned her car ignition on, her mobile chimed away. It was Duncan as she had put his number into her mobile the other day. She reluctantly answered it as she wasn't sure what he was going to say.

"Howdy."

"Raquel, are you going to the shop today?"

"Yes, I promised to volunteer this afternoon. Is this *just* a social call?"

"Sort of. I'll come over there later and why don't we have a coffee together."

"To discuss business?"

"You know I can't discuss my work. But I need to see you."

She tried to disguise her eagerness to see him again, "Really? The shop might be very busy."

"Okay. Well. See what happens. Catch up later then."

Raquel was not sure what that was all about. She decided not to dwell on it for a minute longer.

When she arrived, Bette was neck-deep sorting the town's mail, mainly parcels and doing an online tutorial on delivery procedures on her new tablet. Raquel was partnered with Cindy Mayland.

She found the thin and pale Cindy wandering nervously around the shop, barely visible over the tables of merchandise and fidgeting madly with her limp hair. Some people just travelling through had asked her for coffee but she just froze like a statue. Raquel had not been taught how to use the coffee machine. Fortunately, Bette was situated at the back of the Raindrops Shop. She came out and dealt with the coffee orders.

"Hi doll. How are you doing?"

Bette looked her usual clothes horse best. It appeared that her business struggles were well and truly over. She had packages of her own online shopping efforts coming in daily. Raquel was under the impression that Bette was inspired by

Anabella's vintage clothing tastes, more than she would care to admit.

It's funny how human nature can be curiously perverse. Apart from the locals, the police, the detectives and the law students, the notoriety of the town by way of the murders had brought quite a few strangers and voyeurs to town. In the past, many RVs would pass through but now, they stopped for coffee and cake to hopefully eavesdrop on a juicy titbit of information. Many of these visitors picked up a souvenir at the Raindrops Shop, usually an umbrella. It made for a great talking piece as they travelled around Australia, telling people they had visited the new murder town.

On this day, Bette was proudly holding her new bright pink Prada handbag casually over her arm and wearing a Vivienne Westwood vintage suit with an exaggerated bustle. Her pretty auburn bobbed hair was pinned on the left side by an enamel clip in the shape of a ladies' shoe.

"Good, what about you? I love your outfit."

Bette smiled and nodded her head, "Thanks, doll. It's all thanks to Prada, Westwood and a touch of Chanel. I feel like a totally different woman these days."

Cindy came up to Bette and whispered intently in her ear.

"Oh okay…Cindy tells me that Phil Proctor came in earlier, looking for you."

Raquel thought to herself that would be right. Knowing her luck, she thought she would not see Proctor for the rest of the day.

Bette seemed to be reading her mind again and stated with some confidence,

"The mail hasn't been sorted and he likes to check every day. He'll be back. Anyway, I'd better get back to my tutorial."

At that precise moment, Bette's husband Sandy confidently strode through the front door, whistling loudly.

"Hello dear," he said, outfitted in his high vis gear, scratching his unshaven chin.

"Hi love."

"What's for dinner tonight?"

Bette grimaced and looked at her watch, "Oh honey. I have all this mail to sort out and deliver it on Bridie's old bicycle. You might have to reheat last Thursday's chicken noodle soup. It's in the freezer."

"You know how I hate bloody leftovers."

"Sorry, love. On top of that, I'm putting the shop up on Facebook today, I've started a twitter account so I'm twittering away and I just put five new posts up on Instagram. I have the shop email account set up so I have at least twenty-two messages to reply to. Not to mention, the post office emails. Have your dinner without me, honey. I have no idea when I'll get home tonight."

"Okay. See you sometime."

He walked out of the shop, looking a bit upset.

Raquel kept herself busy, sweeping the floor and dusting the shelves and tables. Cindy was a bit too fragile to do much. However, she managed to water a couple of pot plants outside with a small glass jar.

Finally, Phil Proctor showed up. He rode into town on the splendid black mare. He cut a dashing figure in his dusty Akubra hat and this time, in his brand new red and blue check western shirt and tight moleskin trousers. He walked in like he owned the town.

"Howdy, ma'am," he tipped his hat in her direction.

"Hi Phil," she smiled coyly up at him.

"Have you got time today? I wanted to show you my plans for the town mural."

Raquel looked at Cindy who nodded and half smiled in approval.

"Okay."

"Can you ride?"

"Wh-what?"

"I can go up to McCarthy's place and bring back an extra horse for you. We could ride around the district, enjoy the sunny day. The McCarthy's got a couple of real beauties."

"Okay."

She accepted, liking the idea of spending more time with the charismatic Phil Proctor. With the flick of the black mare's tail, Proctor raced off down the main street. In the meantime, Raquel raced home, which was conveniently next door and found a pair of jeans and a plain white shirt to change into. She found her horsewhip but realised that it hadn't been used for equine pursuits for ages, so she left it under her mattress where she kept it. She found her blue velvet pony club hat and excitedly put it on. It was a tight fit. She fastened the clasp under her chin. She was not sure where the McCarthys lived but she hoped they were not twenty kilometres away.

Thankfully, Proctor returned within the hour, on his proud black mare, leading a tall bay horse, all saddled and bridled for her. He even had a spare dusty Akubra hat for her to wear.

He grinned widely at her pony club hat and proffered her the spare Akubra as a suitable replacement. She reluctantly changed it over. He nodded his approval.

Raquel hadn't ridden since her pony club days, but she remembered the basics. She eased herself up into the saddle and clutched the reins pony club style.

Proctor laughed heartily, leaned over his mount and loosen her tight grasp on the reins, "Here, just relax. We'll do it Western style. No prissy showy horsey stuff, okay? It won't impress me, ma'am."

He wagged his long finger at her and gently tapped the sides of his mare with his boot heels to get her started.

"Gee-up."

She dutifully followed his fluid movements, but her horse seemed to be half asleep. It trotted slowly behind. They were headed to his dirt road, probably for a leisurely ride around the paddocks. But she was wrong. Proctor steered his mare towards the silos and the disused train tracks on the edge of town, and Raquel was forced to follow him nervously up there. She knew it was where the homeless man's body had been found.

He reined in his spirited mare at the base of the high white silos, "I had planned to show you my drawings, but I thought I might best explain it to you."

She was flattered and shy, all at the same time.

He jumped down effortlessly and tied up the mare to a railing which was all that was left of the old Brumby Flat railway station. He then came around to assist her down. His strong spatula hands and muscly arms picked her up again and set her down on the dry, dirt ground very gently.

"Thank you," she breathed, as he still held her tight in his arms. She gripped his arms, feeling the sinewy strength in them. Their eyes were locked together and he pulled her closer. They were so close they could smell each other's scent. She had freshly bathed and sprayed on a touch of lavender oil, while Proctor was a heady mix of dust, women's perfume and masculine sweat.

"Raquel, you are truly a beautiful woman," he said in his usual half-whisper, "I am finding it hard to concentrate right now. I'll be honest with you."

"Well, you did bring me here for a reason. Remember?"

"Yes, ma'am. I should be a gentleman. This is the silos, where I'll be working soon. Because of the murders, I haven't started yet. But the town's decision-makers have been good about it. I have an extra two months staying here."

She nodded, "That's great news."

"Yeah, I would feel a lot better if you could sometimes come here and spend some time with me. While I'm painting. It's a solitary process."

He half let her go. She shivered as he very tenderly ran his fingers up, down and across her shoulder blades under her shirt.

"Sure, I'll drop by and say hello. Now and then."

"I'm mighty obliged to you, ma'am."

Her heart beat faster, it actually felt like it would leap out of her chest as he cupped a warm hand to her cheek and bent forward to kiss her. It was not a Duncan kiss. When Proctor kissed, it was like a slow burn. It ached and touched her to the very depths of her soul. it was a kiss of great life experience and yet utmost tenderness. She put her palm flat against his chest, a signal for him to stop. He reluctantly uncoiled but obeyed her. His kiss had left her breathless.

"I don't think this is a good place to…"

He finished her sentence for her, "…to make out? Listen girlie. That is not my style. Look, ma'am, if you want to be with me, you just have to let me know. Give me a sign. I don't want to pressure you. But I would treat you as the fine little lady you are."

Raquel felt conflicted but allowed him to embrace her for a long, long time. They stood in the shadows of the silos and when the spell between them was finally broken, Proctor was true to his word. He walked her around the perimeter of the silos, his left arm slung casually around her waist and described how his mural would look.

"See? The head of goat number one will be on the corner of the silo here. Then the other two will be on the front, facing forward. The images will be black and white, for that dramatic effect. Which is what I want. Then a bright blue sky."

She nodded, "That will look great. I am just happy you're going to be here a bit longer."

He took her hand gently into his, "Yeah, I am happy too. Lucky the Factory donated extra funds the other day."

Raquel looked puzzled up at him, "What. Factory?"

Proctor smiled, "You know. The Jams and Preservatives Factory."

"No? Never heard of it. Where is it?"

"Just at the end of the street, back there," he indicated with a thumb.

"Oh okay, I'll have to pay more attention to what's around town. I wanted to ask you something else."

"Shoot."

"Why did you come all the way to Brumby Flat to paint the silos? I mean…it's a hell of a long way from New York."

Proctor wryly smiled, "Simple answer. I fell in love. Years ago, I met this famous model from Australia. Well, I guess she was. She acted like she was. It was, like, a fling for both of us. I liked her cute accent, she was tall and a real beauty. She talked about her Australia non-stop and I imagined it's a country full of gorgeous women. Which it is. Anyway, the Tender came up for this place and I thought to myself, here's your last chance to see Australia. And here I am."

"Oh wow."

"True story, my sweetheart."

After a while, they went for a long ride around the district. Proctor seemed to know everything about the place even though he had only been around for a short time. He suggested going to the top of Topham Hill and watch the sunset.

They couldn't stay up there too long as it got dark quickly, so they watched the start of it, before riding back to his cottage. She enjoyed her afternoon with the enigmatic Phil Proctor that she completely forgot about meeting up with the other Phil. She had also conveniently left her mobile phone, uncharged, at home.

Chapter Nine

Local Mayor Mrs Maggie Jarvis lived with her obedient and devoted third husband in the house directly behind Raquel's place.

In spite of her position of power, she was not born to privilege, although she certainly acted that way. She was actually born to very middle-class parents in a town even smaller than Brumby Flat was.

She was the smartest child at her local primary school but when she went to boarding school in Adelaide, she quickly learnt that she was alarmingly what they called a 'little above average student'. She realised that she had to somehow come up on top, the way that cream did. Fortunately, she met her first husband, an up-and-coming criminal lawyer when she had enrolled in a Bachelor of Arts degree, with plans to study archaeology. He introduced her to polite Adelaide society. Then she dropped him for husband number two, a Supreme Court Judge who was wise in the ways of the world and twenty years older than she. He introduced her to a higher echelon of Adelaide society and a vastly improved bank balance. She spent most of her time swanning around friends' swimming pools, being seen at tennis clubs, the Opera, race meetings and all the best golf courses. She learnt to talk the talk. Through her new connections and tireless charity work efforts, she started her slow rise to power.

To celebrate their ten years of marriage, Maggie suggested to her Supreme Judge husband they should go on a whirlwind tour of twenty-two countries in eighteen days. It was quite an itinerary. They had to catch planes, trains, buses, make breakfast, lunch and dinner appointments, make the sightseeing bucket list and celebrate two particularly boozy birthdays on the tour. It all proved too much for her poor older husband who went on the trip to escape the pressures of his 'tight ship' run courtroom.

On day twelve, they had just left Spain and the settling dust of a bullfight behind them. Four hours later they arrived in Cairo, visited the Egyptian Museum where he collapsed over a display case of ancient coins while clutching a chocolate croissant on their run through to the next 'must-see' attraction.

Maggie was very upset when her Supreme Court Judge husband fell off the perch like that, in a foreign country, after ten wonderful years of marriage. She couldn't finish the tour and had to make all the arrangements to return his body to Australia. It was very inconvenient but inheriting the multi-million-dollar estate nearly made up for it.

This time, she had carefully selected her third husband. She really married him for love. Arthur Jarvis did not have a law degree, had no social standing, he was ten years older than she was, but he was a wonderful handyman. He could fix anything around the house. He chased her because he adored her, and she knew right away that he was a keeper.

Mrs Jarvis was busy briskly washing up the lunch dishes in the kitchen sink that afternoon and humming an aria to herself. Life was good. Arthur accepted the fact that she wore the trousers, the boots and the red power suit. He stood about a foot shorter than her but he didn't mind that either.

"Arthur."

Her shrill, strong voice boomed out from their tiny kitchen and seemed to reverberate throughout the house.

"Yes, dear."

Her husband was trying to read the daily newspaper in his armchair in the lounge and was used to constant interruptions. He was, fortunately, able to understand sixty per cent of her conversations and answer them correctly.

"The homemade cupcakes I bought the other day, well, they're still here. Did you want one now with your cup of tea?"

"No dear. But you go ahead, have one or two."

"What are you doing, Arthur?"

"I'm just reading about the town murders."

"Oh yes, what's new with that?"

"Well, the local paper says unconfirmed rumours that the dead homeless man's family came from here, Brumby Flat."

"Oh. I wonder if we know this poor man's family. How intriguing it is, Arthur."

"You know everyone, dear," he mumbled under his breath, propping up his reading glasses.

"What was that? What did you say?"

"I just said…who knows anything, dear. I should imagine it's early days in the investigation."

Lord Mayor Mrs Maggie Jarvis strutted into the lounge, wearing another red power suit but minus her clipboard, balancing his cup of steaming hot tea.

"There you are, here's your favourite. Peppermint tea with a lemon slice. Served on our best Royal Doulton."

"Thank you."

She spun efficiently on her right heel and returned to the kitchen.

"Arthur. I'll take my tea in the kitchen and try this peach and mango cupcake if you don't mind."

"Fine, dear. Yes, you do that."

He managed to read three wordy paragraphs about the plans for the local footy oval to be shared with the javelin throwing Olympic team from Lithuania and the reintroduction of the prestigious Brumby Flat Cup, when he heard his wife bellow out.

"Oh my god, Arthur. These cupcakes are simply amazing. What an unusual taste. I've simply got to have another one."

"Okay, dear. Sounds good."

He turned the page to read more of the story. He was surprised to find out that the timing of a footy match and the Brumby Flat Cup would coincide, if not clash. After a short while, he heard some really loud banging noises coming from the kitchen.

"Are you alright, dear?" he called out.

"I had another two. Oh wow. Wow. So gooood, they are."

He frowned as it didn't sound like his wife talking at all. She was still loud but the words did not seem to flow in the usual way.

"I am going to have another and then I reckon another…yummy yum yum."

"Steady on, dear. Don't spoil your dinner tonight."

He shook his head and returned to his reading. He heard more and more noises, making him wonder if she was clearing out the kitchen cupboards.

"Are you looking for something?"

He heard her laughing heartily, "You shut up. Shut up. Old man, you can shut the fuck up."

"What the hell's wrong with you?"

She stumbled out of the kitchen, in the midst of devouring a cupcake, half of it smeared all over her face. She had stripped down to her oversized, practical underwear.

Her husband turned to look and was horrified at the sight of her.

"What are you doing, Maggie? Have you gone completely crazy? Put your clothes back on, woman," he snapped at her.

She lurched forward and had to steady herself against the back of his armchair. Her eyes were half-closed, her knees were starting to buckle and she was starting to foam at the mouth.

"I am sorry. Too many cupcakes. I think I had six. No, I feel sick. I think I'm sick. Sick of my life. Oh my god. I hate my life. They want this, they want that. They want everything I've got. I'm sick of it. I'm sick. I had six, you know. Six."

She started hitting and slapping herself, as if she was suddenly covered in bugs, crawling all over her. She started to spin around in circles.

Then she writhed, wriggled and hopped about the room madly.

"Oh Arthur," she yelled and howled, "what's all this? It won't go away. They won't leave me alone. They're crawling all over me. Help me, Arthur. Help me."

He got up, reluctantly put his newspaper aside and studied her more closely.

"Maggie, have you been drinking?"

"Help me, Arthur. What the fuck is this on me?"

She pointed to her bare legs but he could not see anything wrong. She wasn't making any sense to him at all.

"I need another cupcake," she cried out suddenly, stumbling past her perplexed husband, back towards the kitchen but she didn't quite make it. She fell forward, face down into their brand new cream shagpile carpet. Because of her height, it was a substantial fall too. The heavy fall broke her nose instantly, as there was less shag and more hard floor in the part she actually hit.

She was now completely silent. A side of her that he wasn't used to.

Arthur anxiously stepped forward, "Maggie? Maggie dear?"

He leaned over her, and finally knelt beside her head. Her listless eyes were staring out, blood was oozing from her nose, her thin lips covered in white foam and she didn't seem to be breathing any more.

He was startled by what had just happened and realised that it was time to call triple O immediately.

Soon after the ambulance arrived, Lord Mayor Maggie Jarvis was pronounced dead at the scene. For the next five hours, the local doctor, police, forensic personnel and the two Detectives from Adelaide descended on the Jarvis's home, combing the place for answers.

****

"Death by hash. Unbelievable," Duncan remarked, looking intently down at Detective Longmeil's scrawled notes. They were both old school. They always entered their written reports later onto their laptops. They were standing together, comparing notes in the Jarvis's loungeroom, a new crime scene.

"Hmm. Hash cupcakes. But I think they've been laced with something else too. You don't normally die from eating five or so hash cookies…or cupcakes."

"Well, technically you don't. Mayor Jarvis is the exception, by the looks of it."

Longmeil nodded, "The rest of the cupcakes have gone off to the lab. Hopefully, they'll analyse it quickly enough and tell us what the other deadly ingredient was."

"Unbelievable. Now we have three murders to figure out in Brumby Flat. What the hell's in the water? What's with this quiet little town."

Longmeil shrugged his shoulders, "I don't know but I need to go home this week. My wife's getting anxious. The kids are running around and driving her bloody crazy apparently."

Duncan smirked, "I'm starting to like this place a bit. But the murder count is really doing my head in."

Local Constable Banner walked up, his hands characteristically on hips and grimaced. He had some important news for the city detectives. He wasn't happy to have unsolved murders in town, but he had to admit it had lifted his profile in the region. In the past, his work had consisted of the odd traffic violation, lost or stolen livestock and nasty harvester accidents. Now the murders had locals jumpy and he was often called to escort the elderly across the only pedestrian crossing in town and to escort the school bus of children to and from their school. And on one or two occasions, he had to break up an ugly coffee queue push and shove episode in the busy Raindrops Shop. He was the undisputed beacon of authority in the community.

"What is it, Constable Banner?"

"Well, detectives, we've just finished taking a statement down from Arthur Jarvis. I thought you should know. He said that his wife purchased the cupcakes from the Raindrops Shop in town."

Duncan sighed and scratched the side of his nose, "Oh my god. It's got to be the Williams woman. The one who wears the old, fancy vintage clothes. She bakes goods for the shop."

His colleague added another note in his notebook, "They do say around here, she makes killer cakes."

"She definitely does. We'd better talk to her."

"What about the others in the shop? They might've baked this time."

Duncan shook his head, "I doubt it. I have it on good authority that one of them can't even make a salad. The other one is too busy running the whole town at the moment. But yeah, you're right. We'll have to interview the lot. Can't do half a job. Still, I reckon we should see Williams first."

Longmeil sighed, "But why kill the lady Mayor? What do you think she had to gain by doing that?"

"I was thinking…could it be an accident. I mean, this is not like the two other murders."

"So, an accident really. Maybe?"

"Could be. We'd better go talk to her."

Detective Duncan knew it wasn't going to be easy talking to Anabella Williams. It was another highly charged, emotional encounter which seemed to be quite the norm with the people living in Brumby Flat.

Anabella had answered her front door which was painted bright lolly pink in her orange nylon dressing gown, wearing fluffy orange slippers with a square light terry towel keeping her hair perfectly in place and a green oatmeal facemask. Duncan was a bit shocked by the sight of her but knew he had to take it in his stride. Detective Longmeil looked at her a little more critically.

"Mrs Anabella Williams."

She blinked at him over her smudged green cheeks, "Yes, you know who I am, Detective. Can I help you? Do you know what time it is? Isn't it a bit late to be knocking on people's doors?"

"We're here on a serious matter, Mrs Williams."

She looked indignantly at the pair of them, "Do you want to come in? The mozzies are out and about. I don't normally open my door at this time of night, but you were persistent."

"Thank you. Well. Yes, we really need to talk to you."

"Come in," she ushered them into her dining room which had a huge buffet full of expensive nineteen-fifties crockery. She was secretly glad she had cleaned her kitchen very thoroughly before they turned up.

Detectives Duncan and Longmeil sat uncomfortably opposite to her. The chairs were hard and the springs were obvious against their rears.

"Mrs Williams, do you always bake for the Raindrops Shop?"

She knitted her eyebrows, "Yes, I do. But only recently, when it's become so busy. What's this all about?"

"You cook every day, do you?"

"I guess I do…I don't know, perhaps. It depends if I have the time. I love cooking. My husband loves my cooking. I cook old style."

"Oh good. Now, did you bring cupcakes into the shop two days ago?"

She thought hard, "Yes, I did. I think it was my husband's favourite. He loves my peach and mango cupcakes."

"And where is your husband?"

She leant back against her seat, looking annoyed. "Why…he's always here with me," her voice started to quiver a bit.

"Where is he?" Longmeil persisted.

Anabella looked like she was going to burst into tears, but she kept her composure, "He is here. Around. And you should perhaps open your eyes."

Duncan waved his hand, "That's enough. It's okay, Mrs Williams. We know exactly where he is. It's not about that. Just need to confirm that you brought in a batch of peach and mango cupcakes two days ago."

She nodded, "Yes, I am pretty sure I did. Why?"

Duncan took a deep breath, "There's been a death. Apart from Bridie Browne and a homeless man, there's just been another one."

Anabella felt her cheeks going red under her green facemask, "You mean, another murder? Is that why you're here? Oh my god."

"Yes. Sad to say but Mayor Mrs Maggie Jarvis passed away this afternoon. She ate a number of your cupcakes and looks like it may have caused her sudden death. We know what was in the cupcakes. I presume you know all the ingredients too."

"It was only peaches, mango, flour...oh," she suddenly fell quiet.

"There were a couple of more interesting ingredients. Why did you want to kill Mayor Jarvis?"

"I didn't...I didn't intend to kill anyone. It has to be an accident."

"But they were your cupcakes, weren't they? I mean, you made them here, you baked them and then took them to the Raindrops Shop to sell."

She bit her lower lip to prevent it from quivering. Then she burst into tears and shrieked. Duncan waited patiently for her to calm down.

"Okay, okay. Someone brings me the hash. I bake them up as cookies or cupcakes, depends on what they want. They come back and just take it away. They pay me in cash. It's a cash deal, okay?"

It was more information than Duncan had expected to get from her. Longmeil was leaning forward in his chair, hands clasped like he was about to engage her, but he didn't.

Duncan took a deep breath and continued his line of questioning.

"So this person or people supply you with hash and any other drug to make baked goods for them. Is that correct?"

"Yes. I wouldn't know...how to get that stuff myself. They just want it made. I just bake the product for them. I am not a drug supplier."

"But you are, Mrs Williams. In a sense, you are. You are taking money; you are supplying these to someone who sells them on."

She said nothing, looking down at the carved teak dining table.

Duncan sighed and shook his head, "You appear to be so respectable, Mrs Williams. I don't understand why you would do something crazy like this. Why do you even need to?"

"It's not cheap to look this good," Anabella started to sob, her voice barely audible.

"What do you mean, Mrs Williams?"

She regained her composure after a few moments, "Vintage dresses, original ones are expensive to buy, you know. Everything I want to buy is priced from fifty to three hundred dollars each. It's a lot of money. But honestly, I didn't intend to kill anyone. It's just some hash. Only hash. I didn't think anyone could die from it."

"Well, this batch had hash, plus another two deadly ingredients mixed in. And this is what caused Mayor Jarvis's death."

"Who is your supplier?" Longmeil piped up.

Anabella said very quietly "I think I need to get myself a lawyer. I don't wish to talk anymore."

Then she cried uncontrollably, tears cutting slimy trails through her green facemask.

Duncan sat far back in the chair, looking quite satisfied. At least he got to uncover her dirty little secret which paid for her expensive taste in vintage wear.

Chapter Ten

Bette was already at the Raindrops Shop early the next morning, starting the mail sorting process. She was very tired as she had received a distressing late call from Anabella the night before. Then she had to send urgent messages to all her volunteers to come in for a special emergency meeting. She was still trying to get her head around various online courses for post office management, keep the accommodation options at her home ticking along and trying to fit in housework and other chores to keep her Sandy and cat Pandora happy. She was grateful that her volunteers were managing to do ninety per cent of the work required to keep the doors of the Raindrops Shop open.

In the last week, coffee orders alone amounted to four hundred dollars. However, Bette was too exhausted to celebrate. Usually, she was dressed to the nines, but this particularly hectic morning, she had poured herself into a black glitter nineteen-seventies jumpsuit. Her auburn hair was unbrushed and sticking up at the nape of her neck. Gold glitter slide shoes completed her look. The jumpsuit was her latest online purchase.

She quickly cleaned the coffee machine while she waited patiently for her shop volunteers to appear. Raquel was the first one to arrive, flopping into a café chair. She was smiling broadly, which didn't exactly match her body language.

"Hi doll. You look like you have some interesting news."

"Yeah, I sure have."

"Hmm. You're starting to get an American twang to your voice. Did you know that?"

Raquel nodded and yawned loudly, "Not surprised if I do. I spent half the night up with Phil Proctor. But no. It's not what you think, Bette."

"I was thinking about nothing. Just got lots of bloody work to do today."

"It was magic. We talked for hours, then he held me in his arms and we watched the sunrise together."

"Well, you've been a busy girl then."

"Nothing wrong with having some good male company. I haven't heard anything from that Detective Duncan. A week has passed. I guess he's not interested in me."

Bette made a face, "I don't think that's his reason for non-contact, doll. From what I am hearing, he's got his work cut out for him."

"He could still just call me. Anyway, Proctor's all over me like a rash, which I am not minding at all. He's so knowledgeable and sophisticated and his accent, like wow."

"Don't be too hard on the poor detective. Now, I have called this meeting to update you all. There's a lot happening around our district."

Raquel raised an eyebrow, intrigued by her friend's choice of words. But her thoughts were interrupted by the sudden quiet arrival of Cindy and the military drill-like entry of Chris wearing his usual army fatigues.

"Hello," Bette said in greeting, indicating a neat row of chairs. Cindy virtually disappeared into hers while Chris sat upright and looked fearless. Raquel was battling to keep her eyes open, slumped far back in her seat.

"Now I've called you all in because we have a situation."

Cindy sat forward slightly and mouthed something inaudibly.

Bette seemed to understand her, "Yes, Cindy. It's a serious situation which affects all of us in this shop."

"What's up, Liz?"

Bette frowned at Chris and said in a matter-of-fact tone, "No easy way to say this. We've lost Anabella Williams."

Raquel stood up immediately, "What? What's happened? Is she dead?" she gasped.

"No, no. She's not dead. But Mayor Mrs Maggie Jarvis is certainly gone, she's dead."

"I don't understand…"

"I am not absolutely certain of this, but Anabella called me last night. Very late it was. She was quite hysterical on the phone, poor thing. Our two detective friends were just at her place, questioning her about the Mayor's death. She said to me she was going to jail. I believe they took her away for more questioning."

"But why?"

"She couldn't say much to me because the detectives were nearby. But I think they believe she somehow poisoned Mayor Jarvis."

Chris shook his head, "That doesn't sound right to me. I know what a killer looks like, and Anabella Williams is not the killer type. And why would she want to knock off the Mayor? She's a real nice lady."

"Anyway, we will be down by one volunteer. We'll have to cope in the meantime without Anabella, which is sad. She's been a great help to us all."

Raquel agreed, "Yes, but once her name's been cleared, she'll be back here."

Seconds earlier, Detective Duncan had slipped into the shop very quietly. He had heard some of their exchange and put in his five cents worth in his smooth, deep voice which could melt butter.

"I don't think Mrs Williams will be back for a little while yet. I didn't mean to eavesdrop on your conversation but there's a lot happening. I think it will take some time to make sense of everything going on in this place."

Everyone turned around to look at Detective Duncan who was standing at the front doorway, dressed in a white shirt, tan trousers with the matching jacket slung casually over his right shoulder. His bright blue eyes studied them behind his glasses. Both he and Raquel exchanged knowing looks, noting how tired they both appeared to be to each other.

"Is that right?" Chris spoke up.

"Just giving you a heads up. I can't say anything more."

"So Anabella's not coming home tonight?" Bette asked.

"No. Most likely it won't be tonight."

He then turned his full attention to Raquel.

"And I need to talk to you for a few minutes."

Raquel yawned again and stretched her arms out, "Of course you do," she mumbled under her breath.

"Let's go outside," he gestured to the door. She followed him.

"Hey, do you know who those people are over there? Do you know what's going on?" He pointed out a group of about ten council road workers gathered around the former post office across the road. They were all busy in their high vis gear and hard hats, pointing their fingers in all directions, studying plans of some sort and some of them were talking animatedly on their mobile phones.

"No idea. Maybe we should see what's going on."

"It's a bloody crime scene they're disturbing," He growled.

He marched over to the closest guy and added his strong voice to the ensuing melee.

"What's going on here? Who's in charge? This is a crime scene area. Can't you see the yellow tape around the building?"

"I'm in charge, mate," piped up a strangely familiar voice, which made Raquel crane her neck in that direction. The crowd of workers parted like the red sea to reveal a short Italian looking guy with wide brown eyes, a pronounced Roman nose, a noticeable paunch and salt and pepper hair peering underneath his yellow hardhat.

"Ricardo, is that you?" exclaimed Raquel.

Ricardo winked back at her, "Hey babe. It's good to see you. Are you fuckin' surprised or what?"

Duncan frowned at her, "You *know* him?"

"Oh well, yeah…he's an ex-boyfriend of mine, but from a long time ago."

Ricardo snorted, looking down at his clipboard, "Long time ago, even. Raquel, I left my dream office job for this construction job in friggin' Brumby bloody whatever so I could be close to you again."

She felt the colour drain away from her cheeks, "I can't believe you did that. You always said to me how you wanted an office job."

"I figured Goliath had to go to the mountain because sure as hell, the mountain wasn't coming to Goliath."

Duncan smiled at Ricardo's analogy, not that he really wanted to. He needed to gain control of the conversation and he achieved it by clearing his throat loudly, "I realise this is a touching moment for the pair of you, but I need to remind everyone that this post office is a crime scene. We had a murder happen inside recently. You do not cross this tape. Now, I repeat. What is happening here?"

"And who's asking?" Ricardo snapped back, holding the official clipboard in front of him, his other hand resting on his hip.

Duncan showed his official ID, "So, what's going on?"

"Local council have plans to run a road right through here. The post office needs to go. Needs to be torn down asap. I have the bloody demolition order right here. See."

Duncan snatched the piece of paper out of his grasp and studied it closely, "I knew nothing about this," he stated.

"Well, the post office was informed about it eight months ago. We got a response back from the lady and she was fuckin' happy about the road coming through. She said she had plans to fuckin' retire anyway."

"Road?"

"Yep mate, a road. A two-lane road. The council wants to divert heavy traffic around the town. Trucks, semi's and all that heavy shit, you know."

Detective Duncan smirked, "Divert? This is the main street. You seem to be diverting heavy traffic right back into the town, not away from it. Let me look at those plans please." he put out his right hand.

Ricardo shook his head and folded his arms over the clipboard, "Naw, buddy. No way. Can't show it to you, mister big city Detective. This is strictly council business."

"The post office lady is dead. Murdered. Are these council people a bunch of twats? Don't they read the news?"

"Hey, I am running this construction bloody show here, mate. And I am following the plans here, to the letter," he tapped his forefinger angrily on the innocent clipboard, "That crappy building's gotta go. The road comes up to here. Anyway, the dead lady didn't own the building. The owners gave the green light. And if you got a friggin' problem with it, I suggest taking it up with the council, righto? Nothing to do with me. Now you can 'f' off, but in a nice way."

Duncan glared at him, staring down his glasses, "Don't worry. I'll sort out the council. I'll be back to put a stop to this…insane stupidity."

Ricardo shrugged his shoulders and winked confidently at Raquel, "Hey babe, I'm staying at the only B&B in town. Room five. Do you want a spare key?"

She said nothing, simply shook her head and walked off behind Duncan.

When they both were standing well away from everyone, Duncan leaned forward and said in a low voice, "I keep thinking about you, Raquel. Since that night we had together. I've wanted to talk to you all week but now, I'm dealing with another possible murder."

She glanced away, "I've been too busy to think about you."

He smirked, "You would say that. I like the way you are. I want to take you out again."

"Again? We haven't had one proper date yet."

"Then I'll just come back to your place this evening."

"You're very confident, aren't you?"

"Come on. You know you had a good time with me."

She turned to face him, "Oh really? Do you think you're the only dick in town?"

"Well…I guess not. There's actually two of us."

"Yeah, that's right," she snapped, but she added about half a minute later, "You just like to joke around. Everything's a bloody joke to you. I'll be home later if you want to come by."

Duncan smiled at her, took out his mobile to deal with the local council and then headed back to his station wagon to catch up on some much-needed sleep in his rented room at Bette and Sandy's house.

Raquel walked back into the shop, to see what other news her friend Bette had for them.

But she had already disappeared into the back room to begin her mail sorting. Chris was working with her today so Raquel started dusting the back shelves. She couldn't see Cindy but knowing her well by now, she might've slipped away undetected.

As she got stuck into her work, she heard the front door swing wide open. It was Bette's husband Sandy who was whistling away. He gave her a small wave of acknowledgement and walked straight past her to the back room.

"Is my honey bunch in?"

Raquel simply smiled and nodded, but happily continued her dusting. Chris was busy polishing some new silverware in the other corner. A couple of minutes later, Bette walked her husband back out. His mood had significantly changed.

"Sorry dear. I've really got too much going on today. It's the end of the month financials, then I'm halfway through an online course on postal banking, and on top of all that, I've got to put the new shop stock up on Facebook, Twitter and Instagram."

"You're never bloody home anymore," he said quite coldly and stormed out the front door.

Bette sighed, watching his back disappear into the distance and shrugged her shoulders, "Husbands. Can't live with them. Can't live without them."

****

Detective Duncan knocked loudly on Raquel's front door at seven o'clock that evening. It took a while before she opened the door, her hazel eyes blinking up at him.

He drank in the sexy scent of her perfume and the long sleeve dress she was wearing with a geometric pattern over it, which barely covered her knees. His heart was already beating quite rapidly when he looked at her. He found her whole being rather exciting, which genuinely surprised him.

"Hello," he said in his strong, musical voice. He had changed into a plain white T-shirt teamed with a pair of navy trousers. His appearance was a little less conservative than usual.

She flashed him a shy smile, "Phil. Come in."

He followed her closely, but far enough to enjoy watching her behind wiggle under her soft dress. She half-turned to face him in the lounge room. He removed his eyeglasses in his usual sweeping gesture, and with his other hand, he roped the small of her back, pushed her hips against his groin and planted his lips firmly on her own. He taunted and teased her lips and rolled his tongue expertly and playfully around hers. She moaned softly, somewhere deep in her throat. He then started to lightly brush his lips over her eyes and her cheeks. He was passionate and needy with his sensuality.

"I want you, I have been thinking about only you. All day." he half-whispered, his left hand gently smoothing her hair, allowing her face to nestle against his shoulder. Raquel found it hard to breathe. She closed her eyes and held him as tight as she could manage. She didn't understand why she was drawn to Detective Phillip Duncan. Phil Proctor excited her, but Duncan was a strange heady mix indeed. As a lover, he could be gentle, aloof and intense, all at the same time.

"Phil," she finally managed to pull away and glance up into his blue eyes.

"What do you want from me? Is it just sex while you are here, in Brumby Flat?"

His eyes glazed over, "You've got me wrong. I think you're amazing. Why are you doubting me again? We talked about this stuff last week."

"It's just that…you've got your job to think of. I can't believe what's happening in this town."

He shook his head and still clutched her sides gently, "I know. I've never had to deal with so many murders in a short space of time. I have a lot to sort out tomorrow. I was looking forward to spending the evening with you. I really need you tonight."

Raquel noticed the sudden change in his voice, his whole mood and leaned forward to lightly touch his forehead,

"What's wrong, Phil? I know something's wrong. Talk to me," she said.

He embraced her tight again, "Tomorrow will be a long, tough day for me. Got that council matter to sort out. And I think I miss being in Adelaide. I've been away from home for so long. But yeah, tomorrow we're doing an exhumation."

"A what?"

"Okay. Put simply, we're digging up a grave."

Raquel widened her hazel eyes, "Oh wow. I guess I can't ask you any more questions about it."

"You guessed correctly. Anyway, let's move on. Let's go have some fun," he took her hand with the intention of taking her to her own bed but Raquel had other plans. She planted her feet firmly and with some reluctance, she pulled her hand away.

Duncan turned around and looked puzzled at her. His eyes were starting to narrow a little without his glasses.

"No. I can't," she said softly, "I mean, we can't. I have actually met someone else. You left me hanging."

Duncan shook his head and put his hands to his hips, "I see. You let me kiss you just a minute ago. I didn't hear you complaining about it either."

"Hey, I don't remember giving you permission to kiss me. You just went ahead and did it. I am seeing someone. You haven't kept in touch with me since that night a week ago. So I don't understand why you expect me to just stand around, waiting for you. I know you're busy but for god's sake, I have my own needs, and desires too."

He picked up his glasses from her coffee table where he had carefully placed them and headed in the direction of her front door.

"So, who is this guy you're seeing? Do I know him? Christ, it's not that creepy road worker today, is it? I thought you had more taste than that."

Raquel hesitated for a moment before she answered him, worried about his next reaction. After all, she reasoned that detectives probably carried guns.

"It's Phil Proctor."

Duncan smirked and rolled his eyes, "Oh yeah, okay. I interviewed him. He discovered the body at the silos. He's that Yankee artist everyone is talking about. Isn't he an old guy? Well. Okay then. I hope you keep enjoying each other's company. Good luck with it."

"Wait."

"It's okay. It's okay. I won't be bothering you again."

He opened the front door to leave and nearly collided with Steve, Raquel's son. They eyeballed each other as they were close to being about the same height.

"Detective Duncan, this is my son," Raquel made a quick, breathless introduction.

Steve's eyes lit up and he put his hand forward to shake Phil's hand. Duncan calmly reciprocated with a strong, firm grip.

"I'm Steve. Nice to meet you. Shit, you're a detective. That must be an interesting job. Police work must be exciting."

Duncan shrugged his shoulders, "Yeah, it is. Can be really long hours but it can be rewarding. You get to travel and get to stay in murder towns, like this one."

"Wow, I can imagine. I'd love to join the police force."

"Nothing to stop you. Maybe you should look into it."

Steve showed off his best lopsided smile, "Yeah, sure. Why not?"

Steve walked in and Phil walked out, slamming the front door firmly shut.

Her son looked at her puzzled and said, "Is it something I said, Raquel? He seems angry?"

"He's pissed off with me, don't worry about it."

"Oh okay. I'm just here to grab some more clothes to take to Nan's."

He walked off into his bedroom.

Raquel stood alone in her loungeroom, left to wonder if she had done the right thing, letting Phil Duncan go a second time.

Chapter Eleven

Detective Duncan looked down at his mobile and realised that he was running a little late for the exhumation. Actually, he was a half-hour late already. He had a restless night's sleep at the local B&B as the law students had decided to take a break from their end of year assignment work and hold a room party. They played music which had the same repetitive beat and talked through the party walls for hours. Quiet had descended eventually at two in the morning which gave Duncan only four hours of dedicated sleep time. All the party evidence was shoved out in the hallway, along with an esky full of empties.

Duncan buttoned up his freshly ironed white shirt and then struggled with his tie in front of the small bathroom mirror. Finally, he mastered it and popped on his glasses.

He walked out into another bright day, twirling his car keys around in his right hand. When he turned the ignition over, he could see the car service symbol flashing up and that he was low in petrol. He realised he had to fuel up at the local service station and it was a stop he couldn't really afford to make, considering how late he already was.

He swung into the service station driveway and pulled up alongside the only petrol pump in town. He filled it up with a twenty-dollar note's worth.

When he went inside to pay, the Nigerian couple behind the counter appeared to be arguing, their voices loud and animated. They were both as tall as Duncan and their skin was as black as coal. They were still wearing their colourful traditional clothing, having only arrived in Australia six months ago. They stopped their animated talking or arguing, and stared at Duncan with their big brown eyes framed by curled black eyelashes.

"Twenty dollar," said the husband in a strong, stern voice. His wife walked away to the other end of the counter, her arms folded defiantly across her colourful tunic. Something her husband said had evidently upset her.

Duncan nodded, producing his wallet, "I have cash."

"Nice day, you think?" the husband smiled, his perfectly white teeth gleaming.

Duncan smiled and replied, "Yeah. Will be a hot day."

He peered at the wife who was observing him through the corner of her eye, as she busied herself restacking some chocolate bars.

"Where do you live?" He asked her, smiling.

She visibly frowned and studied him. She didn't appear to understand.

"Live? Where do you live?"

She nodded her head slowly, "Live here. Back," she indicated pointing a slim long forefinger.

Her husband looked angry at her and spoke sharply in their language. Then he waved his arms excitely at Duncan.

"No. She don't speak English. You go. You go now. Thank you. Nice day to you."

Duncan turned on his heel but as he opened the front door to leave, he cast a quick backwards glance. He saw the husband still waving his muscular arms around and directing her towards the kitchen door.

Once outside, Duncan studied the service station and noticed there were no windows or external doors visible, except for the main shop window and the service station's front door entrance. He made a mental note to himself to run ID checks on the Nigerian couple as soon as he could.

He returned to his vehicle, realising this was the second time he had caught the couple exchanging harsh words. But for now, he had to move it, head out to the Brumby Flat cemetery to see how the exhumation was going. And sometime that day, he also had to find some time to have a word to the local council and ensure the post office was not demolished in the midst of their murder investigations.

He found the cemetery easily, as there seemed to be signs posted everywhere, plus it was located at the end of the aptly named Cemetery Road.

Turning into the gated entrance, he noticed Detective Longmeil's bicycle was already parked there. Longmeil was the new breed of detective coming up through the department ranks, being a soy chai latte with a twist of lime-loving greenie type.

Duncan slammed his car door shut and walked over to the flurry of activity happening at the far back fence. Two gravediggers had been enlisted to help, with local Constable Banner keeping an eagle eye on the entire proceedings.

Duncan took in the fields of red dust and dry, twisted gumtrees around the perimeters of the cemetery. The flies were bad everywhere around Brumby Flat, and he was constantly waving them away this particular morning.

Longmeil was standing there by the fence, overseeing the digging of the gravesite. He nodded acknowledgement at Duncan when he saw him walking up.

"Hey, glad you made it finally," he said with a wide grin.

Duncan sighed, "Don't ask. I guess you've had a good sleep in your bed at home."

Longmeil pulled a face, "Yeah. Not too bad. Laura did nag me about things needed doing around the house but I said not now, honey. I'm neck-deep in murders just at the moment."

"Yeah, tell me about it. You know. I am looking at everyone in this bloody town, and thinking they're a suspect. I have no ideas on this one. Except. I don't think we are dealing with an experienced killer here."

Longmeil agreed with his senior colleague, "Yep. The blows indicate crude, angry movements even."

"Yeah, someone is really pissed off. They're not in control of their emotions. Forced to kill, maybe trying to keep all their secrets intact. We have no murder weapon. Whoever the killer is, they are holding on to their weapon of choice."

"I had a call updating the situation with Anabella, the vintage wearing lady."

Duncan nodded his head, "Good. What's happening there?"

"She's pleaded guilty, but she said she was happy to cooperate with the police. She is willing to assist with investigations, by dropping the name of her suppliers."

"Oh wow. That's good to know. She would not cope well in jail."

"It's going to get hot today. Weather forecast said forty-two degrees."

"Bloody hell. I can already feel it. How's the dig going?"

"Too early to say. Been here for a while but now, I think they're about to make an official start. The soil is chockers with clay and stones. They'll have their work cut out for them today."

"Hey," Duncan pointed to a figure bobbing up and down by the fence line, "Who's that? Are you fuckin' kidding me? Am I seeing things, or is that a jogger, coming this way?"

Longmeil squinted and shaded his face with a cupped hand, "I think you're right, Phil. Looks like the idiot's going to run right through the cemetery. We'll have to stop him."

"Stay here. I'll handle it."

Duncan started jogging himself, back to the front gates. In his spare time, he did a bit of running anyway. As he came closer, he could see the jogger was actually Chris Jones from The Raindrops Shop. He was outfitted in surplus army camouflage T-shirt and matching black lycra pants.

Duncan waved his hand at him, which seemed to have the desired effect. Chris slowed down and stopped at the gates, resting his hands on his knees, catching his breath.

"I'm sorry but you can't come through here today."

Chris started to run on the spot. He frowned and tapped his watch annoyingly, "But I always come this way, at this precise time. It's like my routine, detective. And anyway, my friend Cindy is joining me today. She told me she wanted to take up running. She should get here any minute."

Duncan also tapped his watch, "No one comes through here at this time. It's official police business today. When your friend arrives, I suggest you try a different route."

Chris heaved a sigh, "Well, okay. What's going on here then?"

"You'll have to read about it in the news."

"Not more bloody secrets. This town's full of this secret squirrel shit."

"Looks like your friend has just arrived."

Duncan nodded his head towards the sight of Cindy who was slight and small shuffling around the outside fence in one of her two maroon tracksuits. She looked quite puffed already, although she had just started to jog four metres earlier. It took a while before she appeared at Chris's side, panting and wheezing. It was the most noise that she had made in quite some time.

"Hey, Cindy," Chris said brightly.

She looked up at him and said nothing, dragging her skinny arms up to hang on her thin waist.

"The detectives reckon we can't run through the cemetery today. Police business," he explained,

Well, that made Cindy immediately see red. No one expected the explosion. Her brown listless eyes widened and seemed angry. Her small, narrow nostrils flared and her tiny hands bunched up into fists. She started to scream and jumped up and down on the spot, red dust flying around her feet and ankles. Then she grabbed a substantial tree branch on the hard ground and started smashing it hard against the ground repeatedly. Duncan jumped back and Longmeil looked on, bemused. The tantrum went on for just thirty seconds and at the end of it, not much was left of the tree branch. She then stopped her angry assault, straightened her maroon tracksuit and walked away very calmly.

Chris was left there. He stood straight and still and looked completely lost, confused even. He glanced at the detectives and then jogged off down the hill after her.

"Well. Well." Duncan spoke first and then cleared his throat before continuing, "Wow. I wasn't expecting that. She did a fair bit of damage there."

Longmeil nodded his head in agreement, "Another suspect," he sighed and wrote just the name Cindy into his notebook.

Duncan leaned over to glance at his writing, "So, how many suspects have we got now?"

"Ten, twenty…half the town, I think. Last night I had to add the town drunk to the list. He was in the pub, yelling out he hates everyone and then he started bashing the pinball machine."

****

Raquel was driving towards Brumby Flat in her Pontiac Firebird. She had put in another brief appearance at her workplace and fixed all their IT problems.

It was another warm day, so she had her car windows down to catch any cool breezes. She loved the open country road. She always admired the majestic avenue of gumtrees lining the roadside, whenever she arrived at the outskirts of the town. They created a beautiful high canopy of light and shade as cars drove through. But today she finally noticed how brown, brittle and dry the branches and leaves of the trees were. The drought was starting to take its toll on these majestic gums as well.

She started to slow down as she neared the eighty-kilometre speed sign. It was then that she noticed a tall figure on a horse up ahead, standing in a paddock on the left side of the road. This paddock was empty of trees. The land belonged to the McCarthys. She recognised Phil Proctor astride his glossy black mare.

She only had a moment to glance at him, but she could not mistake his Akubra hat, his Driza-Bone coat, western check shirt and faded Levi's. He recognised her car and tipped his hat slightly in her direction. She saw him turn the mare towards the direction of the town and flick the reins. The mare responded by leaping into an easy canter along the fence line with a swish of her ebony tail. As Raquel neared the sixty-kilometre speed sign, she eased her foot on the brake to slow her car. By then, Proctor and the mare hit their stride and launched into a steady, flat out gallop. They were flying next to her Pontiac and keeping up with her. The black mare's mane and tail were billowing behind her in the wind of their own creation and her dark hooves were thundering across the hard, dry ground. Proctor was guiding her with all the experience of his horsemanship.

He gathered in the reins to slow the mare as they neared the end of the long paddock. Raquel briefly waved to him, her hand out the window as she drove on, into the township itself.

Proctor sat tall in the saddle and tipped his hat again to her. His black mare pranced around in an elegant, tight circle. She looked ready to race again, tossing her head.

Raquel was in awe of Phil Proctor. She held the steering wheel tight and hoped another catch up was on the cards.

Chapter Twelve

The sun was sitting high in the blue, clear sky on yet another dry and dusty day.

The old stone and tin roof farmhouse, surrounded by a line of majestic tall blue gums, dry and brittle bushland shrubs and old rusting farm machinery, looked to be in a state of abandonment. The farmhouse had seen better days. The remote location and the time of the day presented the perfect opportunity for someone to make some mischief.

The farm had been watched closely for a few days and the trespasser knew that its only occupant was busy and away at this time of the day, working on mending fences which the kangaroos or cattle had damaged. The faithful cattle dog had gone off to accompany its owner on their round of farm chores. The only sound to be heard, was an assortment of birds singing, high in the trees,

The trespasser, who was dressed head to toe in black clothing, easily slipped through the rusty open gate and trudged into the large rustic shed where the farm tractor and the old early nineteen-eighties white station wagon was stored.

They knew the station wagon was being used to make weekly trips into town. They had thick gardening gloves on and opened the car bonnet easily. They tinkered away for a few minutes and then closed it again firmly. A layer of dust lifted then settled back on the bonnet, a good indication that a trip to shop in town was well overdue.

The trespasser started to walk backwards. Using a large clean duster taken out from a large black plastic bag, they wiped away traces of their footsteps from the cement floor and stealthily retreated the way they came.

About two hours later, the Range Rover returned up the gravel and dirt track to the farmhouse. The blue heeler was yelping and running ahead of the vehicle, tail wagging.

The old farmer stopped in front of his house and eased himself out of the high cabin of the vehicle. He coughed loudly and then several times for a good, long minute.

"God damn it. I'm past my use-by date," he grumbled to himself, dusting off his denim overalls. He was nursing a fresh, small cut across the centre of his right palm, caused by his intricate work with an uncooperative barb wire fence. He walked with a bit of a limp, caused by a minor tractor accident years ago.

His family had worked the farm for three generations in the district, but he knew he was probably going to be the last. His son and daughter had left the farm years ago, preferring to work in steady city jobs. And his beloved wife had departed the physical world five years earlier.

George Mayfield found it hard to be out there on his own, but someone had to keep the family farm going. He had sold off a couple of the bigger paddocks to neighbours in recent times and the two-year drought had meant that he had to decrease the number of his cattle to a more manageable herd of sixty. He had few visitors, but he had received a phone call from a detective earlier in the morning, asking questions about the recent murders. They said they would be over sometime soon.

After two hours mending one of the back paddock's fences, Mayfield was far too buggered to empty the back of his range rover. As he bent over to pat his excited blue heeler, he started to think about supplies he needed to get from town. The kitchen pantry was starting to run on empty. He looked down at his watch and grunted. He was old school. He didn't own a mobile phone and thought he had no need of one. His home phone worked well enough and if anyone really wanted him, they could wait for him to finish his farm chores.

"Okay, matey, you stay home and look after things. I'll go get us some grub, hey. You're a good girl. Good girl."

He bent over and patted his excited dog.

Mayfield walked through the creaky, rusty screen door of his home and grabbed the key to the station wagon and snatched up his well-worn wallet from the kitchen table.

His dog was excitedly sniffing around the bonnet of his old station wagon in the shed. Mayfield waved her away and started up the car.

He reversed the station wagon which was dusty from the dirt roads and was badly in need of a good wash. He drove down the gravel driveway, happily whistling away. He wasn't interested in listening to the car radio but didn't mind making his own music. He drove confidently onto the dirt straight road to the main highway. It had been recently serviced by a grader, which promised a smoother drive.

A cloud of fine bulldust rose behind his vehicle as he sat smack bang in the middle of the road, driving flat out at eighty kilometres an hour. It was a ten-kilometre drive to the highway and then at least twenty more to Brumby Flat.

He was whistling away and remembered in time that a wicked bend was coming up. He slowed down to seventy kilometres by easing his foot off the accelerator.

As he came around to the bend, he noticed the car sliding sideways a bit more than usual, so he tried to slow it down a little more to keep control. He pushed the brake pedal but nothing appeared to happen. He pushed it again, no response and then started to panic. He was too busy looking down to make sure he was pushing the right pedal, not the accelerator by accident when his back wheels caught the ditch and his car started to careen totally out of control. It hit a large dip in the road and went flying and rolled over three times before hammering into a huge gum tree on the side of the road. The car landed upright. It was all over in a matter of seconds. The dust started to settle but nothing stirred from the battered vehicle. The roof was completely caved in.

About twenty-five minutes passed before another vehicle appeared along the dirt road and happened upon the tragic accident scene.

****

Detective Duncan walked into the Raindrops Shop, intent to finally interview Bette Mitchell. He had talked to a few local residents that week, but nothing new had come to light in terms of his murder investigations. In fact, he still had no clues.

Bette heard the shop door open and peered over her reading glasses. She was seated on a stool at the back counter, where she was sorting some parcel pickups and doing her paperwork. She saw Duncan approaching and quickly stashed away the bottle of scotch whisky and the glass she was drinking from, under the countertop. There was a small 'clink' sound as they touched but she was sure Duncan had not heard it.

She was elegantly dressed in a gold silk Chinese dress with a high collar, her red bobbed hair creating a lovely contrast. She had a set of chandelier earrings to complete the look, which caught the light brilliantly.

"Hello," she said in her husky, dulcet tone, "How can I help you today?"

Duncan made a point of glancing down at his watch, "Aren't you late opening your shop today?"

"Detective, it's Sunday morning. Everyone's at church service. I've been to church already. The shop's not open until midday today."

"Except Raquel," he mused with a smirk. He came over to her and leaned his elbow against the counter. He was more casually dressed than usual, wearing tan trousers with a plain black T-shirt.

"No. She was right there in church, sitting next to me. Looking lovely, as she always does."

Duncan looked a bit surprised and then felt a little ashamed of himself for thinking what he did. He removed his small notebook from his trouser pockets and was poised to write.

"Well, I thought it was time for us to have a little chat. It's long overdue. Been so busy since Ms Bridie Browne was killed."

She nodded, "What do you want to ask me?"

"About the first murder. The homeless man. I know you've heard all the media reports but if you can think back to the time. Before all that."

"Okay, I'll try to put myself there, for you."

"Did you know the Burford family? Or Mrs Burford, maybe?"

"Mrs Burford did you say? No. Not really. I have noticed Mrs Burford a few times in the post office over the last two years. We haven't talked. Hellos and goodbyes mainly. As you know, my Sandy and I have only lived here in Brumby Flat for about two years."

"Did you know that this homeless man was in town?"

Bette stopped her work and stood up, moving around from behind the counter. She looked at him seriously, noting how tall he was. She tripped over something imaginary and had to save the whisky bottle, which then tapped her glass behind the counter. She recovered her balance and leaned against the other side of the counter, looking up at Duncan.

"I guess you should know. I did see him. I saw your Christopher Burford. I saw him arrive in town before he was killed."

Duncan arched an eyebrow, "Really? You've never mentioned this before."

She shrugged her shoulders, "You haven't asked me before, detective," she drew a breath and went on, "I was working back in the shop, it was about after five in the afternoon. I had two boxes of umbrellas I needed to price and quickly put out. Anyway, I think it was about six o'clock maybe. I started to clean the shop about then, and I noticed this car pull up outside the post office."

"What sort of car was it?"

"Excuse me," she emitted a small slightly tipsy hiccup before continuing, "It was an old white station wagon. I have seen it before. Belongs to one of the farmers around here. This homeless man got out, looked around a bit and walked off. He walked that way."

Duncan nodded, "Okay. What did he look like?"

"Who? The homeless man?"

"Both of them actually. Descriptions would be good."

Bette looked thoughtful for a moment, "I think…the farmer lives past Topham Hill, down that dirt road near the rifle range. Someone around here will know his name. Shouldn't you be writing this down?"

"It's okay. I'm pretty good with details."

She paused, thinking hard again, "But the homeless man, Christopher, he was kind of thin, had the start of a grey beard. Brownish hair. I can't remember anything else that night. I only saw him for a couple of moments, then he was gone. Like that."

She snapped her fingers in front of Duncan's face. He flinched and stared at her puzzled.

"Were you alone in the shop? Was anyone else around? That you could see."

"No. I think I didn't see anyone around. Yes. Just me. Of course, that farmer saw him. I saw him arrive. That's it. Hope that helps you out, detective."

Duncan leaned closer on the counter, "Call me Phil. Well, it's better than I've had lately."

Bette folded her arms and sat back down again, "You're talking about Raquel again. I know you like her but you're trying hard not to."

He shook his head and stated, "Maybe you're right, Mrs Mitchell. But she's with this Phil Proctor now. I imagine she's very serious about him. Anyway, I'm asking the questions."

"She's got a massive crush on him, for sure. I think that's what it is."

"I know. She's moved on. And I have to do the same."

"I am sure she likes you too."

"Okay, okay, I've got enough work to do, sorting out all this bloody awful business. Thank you for your information. I'll start my enquiries about the farmer."

There was an awkward silence which descended. Duncan looked like he was preparing to leave, but he leaned in closer again. Bette blinked back at him, her blue eyes as big as saucers. She hoped he didn't get close enough to smell the whisky dancing on her breath.

"Is there something else, detective, I can help you with?"

Duncan's strong musical voice returned, "Where's your husband Sandy today?"

"No idea."

"Not here?"

"Yes. Definitely, he's not here. He would've popped up if he was here."

"You know, I am enjoying my stay at your house."

"Congratulations."

"I see you around."

"Okay," she replied, quite calmly.

"I see you in the cabana, drinking. I see you swimming in the spa. I see you on the tennis court."

"Oh yes."

"I see you are alone a lot of the time."

"Are you still questioning me, as a detective?"

"Maybe. No. I am just telling you what I've observed."

"Is my behaviour of particular concern to you?"

"Yes, it is."

Bette felt the colour rising into her cheeks, and she averted her eyes. It was a touchy, personal subject she had no wish to discuss with a total stranger.

Duncan went on, "Listen. I'm not trying to upset you. I have noticed what you probably don't want anyone else here to see."

Bette got off her stool and half stumbled into the backroom.

"I'm okay. Just go away, please," she called out. She cursed inwardly as she felt the tears coming. She quickly wiped them away and regained her composure after a minute.

She turned around and was startled when she realised that Duncan was standing right behind her. He was studying her face with his own intense blue eyes, framed by his glasses which suited him rather well.

Bette pushed her back against the wall. He noticed that she suddenly looked very small, less confident than she was when he had first walked into her shop.

"I'm sorry. I didn't mean to upset you. I found this by the way," he lifted up the bottle of scotch whiskey from behind the counter, "I'm not judging you but maybe you need to cut down on this stuff. It's not good for you."

"For some reason...I feel compelled to tell you," her voice quivered.

"Tell me what," he breathed deeply. He put the bottle down on a nearby back shelf.

"You might as well know. Sandy and I...I think we're having marital problems. He doesn't seem to be interested in me. I mean, he's attentive to me but there's no intimacy. We haven't had sex for quite some time."

"How do you feel about that fact?"

"You know, you keep on questioning me."

"Hey, you're telling me your story. So, how do you feel about it?" he persisted.

"Unwanted. I feel unattractive."

Inside her head, Bette kept trying to remind herself that Duncan was a man that her new best friend was interested in. But her body gave her real intentions away. She arched her back as Duncan grabbed her hips and slowly pulled her tight dress up to show her shapely legs and curvaceous hips. He heard his mobile ring, but he let it go to message. Bette was perfectly still in his grip. Her breathing had increased.

"Sorry to hear that. You're not unattractive, Mrs Mitchell," he pointed out.

Bette smiled slightly and clutched his arms, "Detective. We don't have time to have great, long conversations. My Sandy might turn up."

Duncan knew what she wanted him to do, but he entertained second thoughts. He wasn't looking for any more complications in his life. He released her hips. He gently and very slowly pulled her gold dress down. He then straightened her hemline of any creases. She cleared her throat, dropped her arms and stepped back.

"Sorry. I don't cut another man's lunch, Mrs Mitchell."

With that, he turned and quietly left.

Chapter Thirteen

After seeing Bette Mitchell and interviewing a young couple staying up at the local caravan park who arrived in town just before Christopher Burford had, Duncan headed back to his room at the unofficial only B&B in town. It was already six o'clock. He passed Ricardo in his hard hat and his high vis gear in the hallway, but they did not exchange as much as a look or a word. Ricardo wasn't happy anyway because Raquel had not come calling. As soon as the road was finished and his work contract was over in Brumby Flat, he figured he would be on his way out of this crazy town.

It had been a long week of investigations, with little in the way of results. Forensics were working around the clock to identify the mysterious body in Christopher Burford's grave. He rang them every day for an update. His work colleague, Detective Longmeil, was having another break at his own home, half his luck. And Duncan's civil talk with the local district council in relation to the town bypass road had descended into a huge disagreement and a volatile exchange. Duncan had learnt that the bypass road was supposed to pass the silos, however, it was nearly half a kilometre off its course and he had great difficulty explaining it to the council. How could they have got this plan so wrong?

He sat on the corner of his bed, cradling an instant coffee made from the service station. It was awful tasting, but he was in desperate need of a caffeine hit. His laptop was sitting on the dressing table, awaiting its punishment. He was always tapping away hard on the keyboard.

He had a quick gulp of the dreadful coffee when his mobile rang. He had saved the number to his phone, so he immediately knew it was local Constable Banner calling.

"Hey, Constable Banner," he answered very casually, "What's new? What do you know today?"

Banner sighed heavily before talking, "Got some news for you. It's not good news, detective."

Duncan replied with reasonable confidence, "Don't tell me. We've had another murder here, in Brumby Flat."

"Well, that was a good guess. I think it's possibly another one, yes. But I'm not one hundred percent sure. It does look suspicious."

"Right. Tell me what's happened?"

"A car's overturned on a dirt road outside of town. One of our local farmers, a really nice old guy. It's old George Mayfield. Anyway, he's dead. It appears to be an accident, he lost control on the road. But there's some scuff marks around the engine. Anyway, I think you should come down here and have a look for yourself. Something's not right. Is Detective Longmeil there too?"

"Naw. He's having some R and R in Adelaide. Okay. I'll head down. Text to me the address."

Duncan hung up and buried his head in his hands. He was starting to think he was never getting home. All he needed was another murder on top of all the rest, that he had no clue about.

Within forty minutes, he was standing at the possible new crime scene. It was daylight saving but the sun was slowly starting its descent. The road was still closed off to all traffic.

"How have you been?"

Banner smiled, "The town's gone crazy, you know. I can't keep an eye on everything but they all here expect me to. Got so many visitors and strangers coming through. I had to escort ducks through the middle of the main street the other day."

"Ducks, really? It's dry as a desert out here."

"There's a couple of ponds around and the local pool. They were a delight to deal with. Compared to these murders. Too many fucking reporters bugging me too. I saw a couple of television reporters walking around the town this morning and stopping people for a bloody story. They'll even make up the story if they have to. No manners, those journos."

Local Constable Banner handed Duncan some official notes to read from forensics' officers who attended the accident. He read through the information quickly and raised an eyebrow.

"Sorry for calling you in so late. But I thought you might want to look into the accident."

"Okay, well. That's very interesting. The accident happened four hours ago. Is that right?"

Banner studied his watch and then outstretched his arm, "Think so. A neighbour found the car, right over there. Looks like it had rolled a few times."

"Dead before the ambulance arrived."

"He was dead before anyone arrived."

"So the signs point to an accident, but it could be a murder disguised. That Williams woman is off the hook. She can't be the killer if she's in the lock-up. You reckon it's a murder for sure?"

Banner nodded, standing in his usual position of authority, with hands on hips,

"Something doesn't add up. One of the investigators said the brakes weren't working. George didn't maintain his farm machinery that great, but his car, I know, was always serviced. Last service was only a month ago at the local mechanics. I did some research earlier."

Duncan made a smacking noise with his teeth.

"Have you got any photos?"

Banner went to his cop car and took them off the passenger seat. Duncan took them and spent time studying the images closely. After some time, he went for a casual walk around the crash site, which was well marked out with tape. He stared at the gumtree which was hit and quite damaged from the impact.

When he finally walked back to Constable Banner, he had a couple of ideas in his head that he needed to pursue.

"Constable, I'll need to use your station as a base for a few days. I have some more investigations to follow up."

Banner nodded his response and followed him back to the other side of the dirt road, "Also, I got a phone call from George this morning. He talked at me, rather than talked to me. He said a detective had called him earlier, asking to catch up for an interview. Do you know anything about it? I just said yeah okay, to whatever he said. I didn't think too much about it, until now. In light of what's now happened."

Duncan shrugged, "No. It wasn't me. Unless Detective Longmeil called him. Doesn't make sense. George Mayfield, did you say?"

"Yes. Surprised you don't remember the name. Mayfield was the coroner for Burford years ago. That was George's younger brother James, you know."

Duncan's ears pricked up, "Really? Didn't he die soon after Burford supposedly got killed?"

"Yeah, his car rolled on Cemetery Road, way back there."

"Hmmm...George Mayfield. He was not on my radar. To interview, I mean."

"Detective, is there anything else you need?"

"Actually, yes, do you have a recent photo of George Mayfield?"

"Found this picture. On the internet," Banner surrendered his mobile for a moment.

Duncan rubbed his sweating forehead and studied the mobile screen closely. He handed it back. As he walked on, back towards his station wagon, it suddenly hit him. He knew who he had to talk to right now.

"Can you please forward his photo to me? To my mobile," he turned and said before settling into his car. Then he took off down the dirt road. He had a twenty-kilometre drive ahead of him.

When he arrived back at Brumby Flat, he immediately ran up to the Raindrops Shop. He knocked loudly on the glass door. After knocking a couple of times, he assumed no one was there. He jumped back into his car and headed back to the B&B.

Along the way, he dialled Bette's mobile.

"Hello?" her unmistakable husky voice answered, which gave Duncan a sense of relief.

"Bette, Detective Duncan. Where are you? I need to speak to you urgently."

"I'm relaxing out back. In the cabana."

"Stay there. I'll be over there in a minute."

"Okay. Sounds very dramatic. Can't wait to find out what it's about, detective."

Bette switched off her mobile and sat back in her cabana. The sun was starting to go down so the chances of adding to her tan had well and truly dimmed with the loss of light. She felt the chill in the air and casually draped her new cashmere floral cardigan over her bare shoulders. She was still wearing her itsy-bitsy barely enough room for a polka dot bikini underneath. She leant forward and elegantly scooped up her chilled glass of whiskey sour. She slowly sipped it and wondered what Detective Duncan's choice of drink refreshment would be.

She removed her aviator sunglasses and released her bobbed auburn hair which was pinned back by a pair of tortoiseshell hair combs.

Detective Duncan finally appeared standing next to her, still in his tan pinstripe suit with a plain white shirt. At just over six foot, he towered above her for a moment. She gestured to the sun lounge beside her and he came down to her level. His glasses glinted in and reflected the last shards of sunlight.

"What's your poison, detective?" she asked him brightly.

He smirked, "Poison is not an expression I particularly like at the moment. What have you got there?"

"Whiskey sour, it's very nice."

"Sounds complicated."

She had another small sip and replied, "It is. Requires a bit of preparation. But I'm happy to make you one if you really wanted one."

"If you have a beer, that's great. That will do me."

She blinked at him, "How boring. The beer's in the mini-fridge."

Duncan turned to look, got up and helped himself to an ice cold stubby.

He could see that Bette was far too relaxed to move. He was also trying hard not to notice her slim bare legs curled up in the cabana and the bikini she was barely covered by. Her full breasts were held up by skinny spaghetti straps. It was an amazing feat of gravity that her nipples were not peeping out of the miniscule garment.

While he tackled his beer, Bette bent over and removed two cigarettes from her slim silver cigarette holder, a recent online purchase. Duncan watched her intently, waiting for a wardrobe mishap. She put them in between her ruby red lips, struck a match and lit both up at once. She handed one cigarette to Duncan.

"But I don't smoke."

She held it there, seemingly suspended at the end of her fine elegant wrist and drew on hers, "I don't smoke either, but I kind of need it tonight. My nerves, you know. Shot to pieces."

He took it from her fingers, and half smiled back.

"Okay, Just once. I must admit. It's been another crappy day here, in paradise."

He drew back and coughed the smoke straight out. Bette laughed. He immediately stabbed it out in the ashtray.

"Not for me," he said, coughing again.

"You're not a smoker, for sure," she mused, puffing away.

"You know why I've had such a crappy day?"

She shook her head, "I'm sure you want to tell me all about it."

"Another murder is possibly on my hands. Christ. Got a serial killer running loose. Oh, and where's your husband?"

"Relax. You can relax. He's driving a big rig to Ballarat tonight. He takes on hauling work sometimes. He doesn't have to but I'm glad he keeps it up."

"The work, you mean?" he remarked.

"Yes, of course, the work. What else?" she blew out a curl of grey smoke.

"Who is still renting your rooms?"

"You are, on the top floor. The law students are gone. I have a council worker now, on the second floor. He thinks he's it and a bit. Funny, short, weird guy. I think a couple of reporters are still around. They are a bit of a nuisance. In and out all hours of the day and the night. Writing their damn stories. Running around the place with their cameras."

"Bette, I want to go back…back to our conversation yesterday. You gave me a description of the farmer who gave a lift to Burford. I have a picture to show you on my phone. Please, be honest with me."

"I will. Of course."

"Is this the farmer you saw that night, when Burford returned?"

Bette leaned forward to study the photo on his mobile. As she leaned in, Duncan noticed the gentle, heaving curves of her tanned breasts.

"Oh my god. That's him. Definitely."

Duncan retracted his phone, "Wow, that's interesting. He's dead. Now he's dead. Died in a car accident this afternoon."

Bette leaned back and nearly disappeared into the shadows of her cabana, with her slim legs just showing.

"You're kidding? It happened today?" she exclaimed, then sipped her whiskey sour again.

"We have his name," he whispered, worried that the reporters may overhear them talking, "But I'm here because I am worried about your safety. You see, the killer has knocked off Christopher Burford, now the farmer who drove him into town and if they saw you that evening too, Bette, well, you could be next."

"You're not serious," she visibly frowned and had another slightly nervous drag of her cigarette.

"Yeah. I am. Lock everything. Keep an eye out for any suspicious behaviour. And I think you should text me where you are, from now on. I mean, I know you're either at the shop or you're here. I know it's not rocket science, where you have to be. But it could make my working life a little easier."

"Please tell me that you have some leads, detective."

Duncan nodded, "I am watching ten people, all locals. But now, I also have to watch you. Makes it more challenging."

"I have Sandy."

"But he's not here tonight. Just do as I say. Promise me, you will be careful."

Bette fluttered her blue jay eyes and polished off the last of her whiskey sour with a greedy gulp, "Okay. I'll try and be on my best behaviour. I hope you're wrong. Maybe it's a coincidence he's dead. You said it was a car accident."

Duncan whispered to her again, "The brakes on his car failed. Someone had a play under the bonnet. I read the report."

Suddenly, there was an awful shrieking noise accompanied by a leaping shadow which landed directly in front of the cabana. Duncan sprung into immediate action and grabbed Bette's closest hand and pulled her out of harm's way, out of her cabana and into nearby bushes. Her floral cardigan floated off her shoulders.

"What on earth are you doing? Are you crazy?" she cried out, pulling her hand free of his and rubbing her arm, "That's just our cat Pandora. She came to say hello."

Duncan clasped her arms and looked over her shoulder. He took in the picture of the now seated and content looking Russian Blue cat with one blue eye, a crooked tail sweeping casually over the cement footpath and with half her left ear missing.

"That's a cat? I'd hate to see your pet dog," he remarked.

Bette looked up at him and frowned, "We haven't got a dog. Pandora is a lovely pet. And we can come out of hiding now. It's perfectly safe."

Detective Duncan leant forward, cupped her face in his hands and planted a quick, firm kiss on her right cheek before she had time to react. He managed a final glance down at her heaving cleavage as he pulled away.

"That's all you're getting, Mrs Mitchell. Keep your nose clean, And your ears open. Have a good evening."

He left her standing in the garden, shaking her head and her hands resting on her hips.

The next morning, the newspaper screamed headlines like 'Murder count rises in Brumby Flat' and 'Profile of the Brumby Flat killer.'

Chapter Fourteen

Raquel was listening to her favourite music CD, driving to the next town to do some grocery shopping, when a call came through her Bluetooth. It was Phil Proctor.

"Hello, sweetheart. What are you up to? Where are you?" his strong American accent was quite seductive.

"Hey, you. Not much. Just going shopping."

"I would love to see you today. Can you come around?"

"For a ride?"

"No. I really wanted to spend some time with you, my lovely lady."

She did not want to seem too eager all the time so she said in her best casual tone of voice, "I've got a couple of things to do today. Domestic stuff, you know."

"Oh, come on. Ditch the apron, sweetheart."

She smiled, "Okay, okay. I'll see you soon, but I'll need to store some things in your fridge and freezer."

"That's fine with me. Come by as soon as you can."

They hung up and she coasted along the freeway, wondering if this was going to be the day when the charismatic Phil Proctor finally made his intentions clear to her.

She arrived at the supermarket and wheeled the shopping trolley as fast as she could through the narrow aisles. She had to dodge other shoppers and the trolley had one crocked wheel on it, so keeping it straight proved a challenge.

She threw her food shopping into the boot and headed back to Brumby Flat. At the last minute, she had grabbed some special goodies, including some chocolate and strawberries.

She arrived at Proctor's cottage in record time. She had unfortunately hit a low flying parrot with her car along the way, but no damage done to her car. The parrot did not fare so well.

When she turned up the no through dirt road to Proctor's, in the rear-view mirror she noticed a white four-wheel-drive vehicle turn off the same way, and then it slowed down and stopped. It was starting to reverse, so she assumed the driver had taken a wrong turn. She was sure the vehicle had followed her all the way from outside the supermarket, but then she thought she might have just imagined it.

She parked her Pontiac Firebird in Proctor's driveway. She took a deep breath, smoothed her floral skirt and knocked on his front door.

Proctor opened it wide, looking disarmingly provocative in his partially unbuttoned western check shirt and a faded pair of tight Levi's. He had his tan brown cowboy boots on. His scent was a mix of Red Door perfume, manly sweat and a pleasant horsey smell. It was another hot summer's day in Brumby Flat but he looked incredibly cool in what he was wearing.

"Howdy, ma'am," he said brightly, slipping his hands in the side pockets of his Levi's. She tried hard not to notice the pleasing bulge in his jeans.

"I apologise for taking some time to come to the door. I was listening to some bluegrass out back."

She followed him into the hallway. He turned to her and shook his head.

"Raquel. I'm sorry I called you over when you're so busy but…I had to tell you something, it's real important."

Raquel knitted her eyebrows, wondering if it was going to be good news or bad.

"What is it?"

Proctor stared at her with his intense blue eyes, faintly lined at the edges,

"Goddamn it, girlie. I am madly, deeply in love with you. There. I've said it now. And I can't figure out what to do about it. I know it sounds a little crazy, but are you on the same page? Or not? Are you? I need to know how you feel. Do you feel anything for me?"

Raquel sighed in relief. It was the words she had wanted to hear from him.

"Yes, I think I love you too," she then added quickly, "Look, I have to tell you about my son."

"Your son?" he raised his eyebrows, "You've never mentioned you had a child."

"Phil. He's a grown-up. He's not little, little. He works and he lives with my mother at the moment. I told him to stay away from here. Too dangerous for him to stay here because of these murders."

"I see." He looked at her critically.

She could tell his mood had changed, so she decided to recount some of her life story to Proctor.

She told him she was born in Adelaide and it was an ordinary family life until she turned eight years old and her mother took her to see her first-ever circus. The circus always set up in a reserve just down the road from their house.

She fell in love with all the magic, the glitter and sequins and especially the high trapeze. When she went home that afternoon, she proudly announced to her conservative father that she was going to join the circus one day. He wasn't happy and firmly told her that her ambitions would change many times before she grew up. But ten years later, after she completed high school, she was true to her word and ran away to the circus when it magically reappeared at the local reserve.

She had met and fallen in love with Mischief the clown who was a special guest performer of the circus, direct from Madrid, Spain. He was mysterious, dark, handsome and had an amazing tan under his clown makeup. He offered her the chance to learn all about the world and share a berth in his plush four-star caravan. He had second billing at the circus which was pretty good for just a clown. The second billing was significant as he had a world-renown reputation. If he wasn't happy with something happening at the circus, he'd make a big deal about it. She liked the fact that he seemed to be in control of the topsy-turvy world around him. And he was quite the romantic too, forever finding coins and daisies in her hair, behind her ears and making them magically appear in the palms of her hands.

After Raquel had mastered the basic acrobatic skills needed for the trapeze, the art of quick costume changes to support other acts and finished a whirlwind tour of Australia,

Mischief the clown announced that he was returning to Europe. He asked her to go with him to feature in an international well-known circus troupe. She only agreed to go as he could speak twelve languages and she was sure he would look after her in these strange foreign countries. Moreover, she thought that he actually did love her.

But when they arrived in Europe, Mischief became quite selfish and declared to all who bothered to listen and stated in advertising 'Monsieur Mischief celebrates his triumphant return to Europe.' Raquel was merely billed as one of the 'Flying Byrds' of the trapeze. She saved all her money as they toured Europe for the next two years, but it all came crashing down, literally, when she missed the catchers' hands and bounced off the safety net. Mischief visited her every day during her short stint in hospital, presenting her with his circus act flowers from his sleeve and wetting her face with the flower on his lapel. That way, he saved on flowers because he didn't need to buy her any, or so it seemed to her romantic heart which was slowly breaking.

While she recuperated in his caravan from her knee operation, she announced to him that they were going to have a baby. Mischief the clown suddenly had a long, sad face and she realised that he was not that happy about the prospect of becoming a father.

She eventually rang her mother from a phone booth in Prague and said she was finally coming home. She left Mischief the clown to do what he did best, which was entertain children around the world over.

She returned to Adelaide, completed an eight-week IT course and worked in a call centre for the next twelve years, raising Steve with the help of her mother.

Proctor had listened intently to her story and nodded.

"Well, that's okay. I hadn't expected that you had been in a nunnery all your life. At least you haven't told me that you're a three-headed, fifty-foot-tall woman from outer space. Mind you, that would be fascinating too," he said, winking at her.

"Are you upset with me?"

"No. Not at all. I reckon it's really cool that you have a son. I have a son too but he works in LA. He's far too busy to spend any time with his dear old dad."

"Steve's a beautiful son."

"I don't doubt it. You're a beauty," he said softly, "Come here, my young lady."

He took her hands in his own and leaned forward to kiss her forehead. Then he softly kissed her eyelids. She shivered under his light, sensuous touch. She secretly hoped that he wasn't going to stop.

He placed her warm hands against his chest with its few stray, curly grey hairs peering over his unbuttoned western shirt. One arm pushed her up against his groin and his other free hand threaded through her silky blonde hair. His breath came hot and heavy and his nose flared. He kissed her top lip and teased it. She started to gasp and she felt her pussy heating up. He rubbed his groin against her. She could feel him getting hard exactly where he needed to be.

He suddenly bent over and scooped her up easily into his strong arms. She moaned deep in her throat and clasped her hands around his neck in surprise.

"Oh my god," she exclaimed.

"Save it. Tell me how good I am *after* we make love," he whispered, nibbling her left ear playfully and effortlessly carrying her off into his bedroom.

He knelt down and placed her gently on the edge of his queen-sized bed. She sat there, looking up at him as he unbuttoned the remainder of his shirt and took it off.

"Allow me to help you," he breathed, his long, slender fingers releasing her shirt buttons with the ease of experience. He then took her left bra strap off her shoulder and kneeling, he kissed and gently teased her nipple and then moved onto the underside of her soft, creamy breast. She shivered under the electricity of his gentle, seductive touch. Then he lowered her down so that her blonde hair brushed his quilt cover and pulled her legs sharply towards his groin. Her pussy was now raised on the corner of the bed and he was leaning over it. He flicked her skirt up to her waist and noted that she was wearing no underwear. He could smell her pussy, he could feel it was a hot spot, aching for attention and his hungry mouth went down on her, his head disappearing between her creamy thighs.

"Oh fucking god," she squealed out her delight and closed her eyes. She had definitely found her 'Mister close to perfect'.

****

Five hours later, Raquel and Phil Proctor were lying naked together within his fine Egyptian cotton sheets, her head resting on his tanned right shoulder. She had just finished giving him a blow job so he had a satisfied expression on his face and his eyelids were half shut.

"Well, you're a surprise package for sure, my sweetheart."

"Oh shit," she cried. "Just remembered. I left all my shopping in the bloody car."

"It's okay," he said, gently patting her arm, "I'll give you some cash to replace it."

"What's New York like?"

He propped himself up on his elbow, looking at her, "It's a magical place, my New York. You can be surrounded by humanity, and yet you can find places to be alone. Central Park is amazing."

"Phil?"

"Yes, ma'am."

"I guess you have an idea who the killer is? Do you? You said you did before."

Proctor nodded his head, his ruggedly handsome face twisting to look at hers, "I have a couple of ideas. No proof yet. And no one's paying me money to identify killers anyway."

She leaned across and gently punched his shoulder, "Be serious for a minute. If you know something, you should be telling the police. My friend Bette. She thinks she's in danger. She rang me this morning, all stressed out."

He smirked, "Or so she might think. I reckon I saw something that night, when the stranger showed up. Now that's saying too much, as it stands. You don't want to know the rest of it."

His face came even closer and his breath came hot against her left cheek as he gave her a quick peck.

"Phil," she said nervously, "I wish you would understand. Three people are dead, murdered. Anyone of us could be the next to go. You should be thinking about Bette's safety, mine, or at least, your own."

"Hey, I care about you, Raquel. That's why it's better for me to keep my thoughts to myself. If you're so worried, spend more time up here with me. You're perfectly safe here with me."

She snuggled her head into his chest. "I know. I do trust you. It's just that I can't trust anyone else in town."

"Hey, I reckon your friend Bette's okay. What about the detectives? Anyway, you can move in with me for a while. I don't mind. I'd love to have you over here."

Raquel smiled, "Phil. I can't cook very well and I'm not good at cleaning either."

"You're good at, let's just say, other great things. And you hug me real nice too."

"You know," she narrowed her hazel eyes and said in a half-mocking tone, "you could even be the killer."

He laughed heartily, "Love your sense of humour, sweetheart. And before I forget, I wanna take you to the local rodeo. I think it's coming soon."

She draped her right arm over his strong, heaving chest, "Okay. I'm up for it. I think."

"Say. What's that noise?" he carefully placed her arm to the side of the bed and sat up to peer through the bedroom window. The wind had picked up outside, the windowpane started to rattle and he could see the sky had turned brilliant shades of red and orange.

"It looks like another dust storm rolling in."

Raquel reclined back on her pillow, one arm provocatively raised above her head, "Looks like I'm not going anywhere tonight," she mused.

Proctor smiled and returned to the bed, embracing her in his sinewy, tanned arms. He started kissing her lips slowly and tenderly, cupping his right hand under her chin and she knew another round of passionate lovemaking was about to commence.

Chapter Fifteen

Detective Duncan was making a return visit, coming up to the low white picket fence of Mrs Elaine Burford's home. It was another stinking hot day but he knew this occasion required his best tan suit, complete with a white pinstripe shirt and his only tie. He was sweating profusely from the relentless heat, but he had an important job to do today.

He studied the front garden closely as he made his way up the footpath and noted the rosebushes had dried out and the lawn was now full of overgrown weeds. Since his last visit, the garden had fallen into a neglected state, along with the peeling exterior of the house. He knocked briskly on the front door of the gentleman's bungalow and a few seconds later, he heard slow footsteps echoing down the long hallway.

The door opened just a fraction, and a familiar-looking elderly lady peered out through the broken screen door and looked up at him.

"Hello. Oh, it's you. You're back again?"

"Yes, Mrs Burford. Senior Detective Phillip Duncan. From Adelaide."

He lifted up his badge and ID for her to see, "I need to talk urgently to you."

"I was expecting Meals on Wheels again, not you. Come in, detective."

She unlatched the creaky screen door and he followed her shuffling, hunched figure through the hallway into the cluttered front lounge room. She had difficulty reclining onto her three-seater club lounge but finally managed it. As she had done on his previous visit, she balanced her reading glasses on the tip of her nose to return to her knitting. She was still dressed in a faded floral housecoat and wore glittery bed socks on her feet, instead of the unicorn slippers she had been wearing last time.

Duncan sat down on the other end of the couch.

"You have more news for me, detective?"

"Yes. As we discussed a while ago, we went ahead with your kind permission and dug up the body in your son's grave."

She stopped her frantic knitting and peered at him with her grey, crinkled eyes.

"Well, I want to know everything. I need to know what happened so long ago."

He took a sharp intake of breath, and continued in his lyrical tone of voice, "We have formally identified the body in the grave as eighteen-year-old Tom Lee Munroe, who lived in Newcastle. I believe he was on a road trip around the country."

She frowned, "Munroe? There was no Munroe in town, I recollect."

"I believe he may have hitchhiked his way into town and tried to steal a car. Unfortunately, I can't verify that information with your son. So we are assuming Tom Munroe tried to steal your car at the time he was here, in Brumby Flat.

And while escaping, he accidentally rolled the car on Old Emu road and I believe your son Christopher found him dead and made the identity switch."

"I see."

"Now, Mrs Burford we have to go public with this information. The profile of your son's killer suggests they are keen to keep this a secret. Whoever it is, must've been with Christopher when the identity switch was made."

She frowned and let her knitting occupy her hands again, "I don't know about this. Going public? It's bad enough…well, I mean, what will people think of our family? Don't you think they'll see how bloody silly we look, Glen and I, not being able to identify our own son? And burying some complete stranger in his grave? Oh no. It's not a good idea to go public."

Duncan could see that he was up against it. She had become stubborn and set in her ways. So he decided to play the best hand he could and tried a different tact with her, as he had done on his last visit.

"Think of your Christopher. Don't you want his killer to be brought to justice? You were led to believe, all these years, that your son had died in a fiery car crash. Someone close to him covered everything up. His killer walks this earth right now, unnoticed. Why let them continue to walk free?"

"I understand that, detective," she replied, not skipping a beat with her knitting, "Of course, I want justice for my son. For me. Whoever it is, they took my precious son away from me. He was dead to me for over thirty years and if only I had known he was alive that long, things could've been so different. I think about that every single day. Fortunately, I have my faith to help me through."

Duncan nodded his head solemnly, "Yes, I understand. Now, I need you to think back over thirty-two years ago, before the car crash happened. I need to know who Christopher's friends were. I think that's a good place to begin. Someone around here did help your son to leave town and he took up Tom Munroe's identity. We are sure about that."

She sighed heavily and put her knitting to one side. She raised herself from her seat with some difficulty and leaning over, she fumbled under her coffee table. She held up a dusty old photo album and handed it directly into Duncan's outstretched hands.

"Here are my Christopher's photos, his friends are all in there, but I can't remember all their names. It was ages ago, detective, but I'll give it a go."

He smiled and opened the buckled pages. Straight away, he turned to a faded photograph with four youths dressed in mid-nineteen-eighties fashion. Duncan recognised Christopher right away who was smiling broadly and leaning back on the bonnet of his Ford Falcon XY, arms crossed. Next to him on his right, was a girl with long blond hair and a big toothy smile in a pink fluffy jumper and wearing tight pink bubble-gum jeans, leaning on his shoulder. To his left, there were two young lads wearing casual T-shirts and jeans. They were standing awkwardly with their hands stuck in their pockets. They looked like a couple of country boys.

He leaned over to Mrs Burford and pointed to the photograph which was faded and tinged with orange hues, "Are these Christopher's friends?"

She put on her reading glasses and after a moment, she said, "Yes, they are. Well, I think I remember two of them.

That girl there. Her name was Alison Walters. She was the popular girl at high school. My Christopher had a big crush on her. He told me that once. But she wasn't interested and liked him as a friend, I think. She seemed like a really nice girl."

Duncan took out his notebook and jotted her name down.

"And where is Alison now, Mrs Burford?"

She shrugged her shoulders, "I don't know. Last I heard, she married a local farmer and they moved away to Orange, New South Wales. Her family left the district about ten years ago and I don't know what happened to them."

Duncan pointed again to the photograph and leaned forward, "What about these two boys? Who are they? And where are they now?"

She frowned and studied the picture hard, "Well, I don't remember that one," she indicated the one on the far left, "But this one here, standing right next to my Christopher. That is George Mayfield's son."

Duncan suddenly straightened in the club lounge and pushed up his glasses on the bridge of his nose, "Oh wow. Are you sure? That's Mayfield's son?"

She tapped the faded photograph, "Yeah, that's right. We all called him Bobby. Bobby Mayfield was Christopher's best mate. Used to infuriate me because he ate so much. He was always at our place, helping himself to dinner and whatever we had in our fridge. When my Christopher died, he seemed to take it really, really hard. He stopped coming around and left town about a year later. I believe he moved to a small town in Victoria."

Duncan took his notebook out of his shirt pocket and started writing.

"So Bobby went by the name of..."

"Robert. Robert Mayfield," she replied in a crackly tone of voice. She started to sob quietly then, "Poor old George Mayfield. I was sad to hear about his passing. Bobby never ever came to visit him again. He seems to have disappeared now, but I remember George saying he would call him up for birthdays and Christmas and wish him all the best. He had no interest in the family farm, by the sound of it. George never changed his phone number, just in case his Bobby called him."

"And what about this young lad here?"

"Sorry, detective. I don't remember his name. He still lives in town, I think. But I'm not sure. He only hung around because he liked the girl. He wasn't around Christopher for very long."

"Thanks, Mrs Burford, you've been very helpful. By the way. Did this Bobby, would he have had a huge influence on your son, do you think?"

She reclined her grey head slightly, "Maybe. They were as thick as thieves. Those two were very close. They were pranksters, the pair of them."

Detective Duncan looked long and hard at the Mayfield's lad. He had a mop of long light brown hair and a lopsided grin. His eyes were closed from a mirth shared by this group of friends when the photo was snapped. Duncan glanced through the album but couldn't find a photo which actually showed Bobby's eyes. In all the photos, Bobby was in profile, standing behind someone or his head was turned away.

"May I borrow this photo?" he tapped it.

"You may."

"Thank you. I'll look after it. I promise."

****

The Raindrops Shop was busy as usual that morning. Bette had arrived early, changing around the table displays, pricing the two new boxes of vintage-inspired umbrellas which had just arrived and checking in the new parcels. Bette was rushing about the shop in her latest online purchase, an Evelyn Neis drop-waist lace dress. She had a matching pink silk bow tied in her shiny bobbed hair. In the era of the nineteen-seventies and nineteen-eighties fashion, she seemed to have found her groove.

A pile of daily newspapers arrived on the veranda and she opened the door briefly to drag them inside. Then she returned to her parcel sorting.

She heard a loud rapping on the front window and saw Raquel waving enthusiastically at her. She hurried back to the front door.

"Come in, doll. How's the grand love affair going?"

Raquel felt her cheeks flush red, "Oh god. Can't really talk about it, you know. But I am so happy."

"Good for you. Now, have you got some free time to help me? I have to open the shop in ten minutes and I'm a little bit behind."

"Yeah, okay. I can spare about an hour."

Bette nodded, "Well, Chris should be here by then. That would be a great help to me. The reporters will be in soon, lining up for their morning coffees. I'll be back soon. Can you please manage things? You're a treasure, doll."

Raquel watched on in puzzlement as Bette disappeared into the back room. She then shrugged her shoulders and opened the front door for business. As she brought out the A-frame shop sign for the front pavement, she saw Bette quickly whiz past on Bridie's old bicycle, with a basket full of town mail, her lace dress bunched up and hitched up around her lithe thighs. A bike helmet was loosely thrust over her perfect bobbed hair with the chin strap looped, rather than fastened tight.

Her friend proved to be right about the reporters swarming around the town, on the prowl for new stories and new angles on the murders. They descended on the shop like a locust plague. Raquel had finally mastered the temperamental coffee machine and she produced an exhausting series of lattes and cappuccinos. The reporters stood around in a long, winding queue, forced to make uncomfortable conversation amongst themselves. Everyone was after an exclusive headline and no one wanted to give up any crucial information. A couple of them tried to question her but she shrugged her shoulders, saying she wasn't a local.

When Bette returned from her mail delivery, she immediately took over the coffee orders and thanks to her experience, she had the last of the reporters out of the shop within fifteen minutes.

Raquel was kept busy at the merchandise counter as travellers stopped in to buy a postcard or an umbrella. Chris did not turn up which was unusual for him, so Bette asked Raquel to stay on for an extra hour.

The coffee orders finally thinned out, and Raquel had a chance to sit down at a café table and read the newspaper over a soy chai latte she had made for herself.

"Did you read today's paper?" she exclaimed loudly when the shop was empty.

Bette shook her head, "No doll. But I guess it's all about the murders."

"It's unreal. There's like five pages devoted to Brumby Flat and the murders."

"Well, what's the latest?"

"The front page says 'Thirty-two-year-old mystery unearthed'. There was some guy called Tom Lee Munroe found buried in Christopher Burford's grave. Wow. Can you believe they kept a secret like that buried for so long? And they also mention Lord Mayor Mrs Maggie Jarvis. No state funeral, but they say here that they will hold a special memorial service for her at the Brumby Flat town hall next week. They expect hundreds to attend."

Bette raised an eyebrow, "That's very nice. No surprise there. She was well known in the district, so that makes sense," she suddenly spun around, "Hey. What was that name you said? That guy they found in the grave?"

Raquel skimmed over the page, "Tom Lee Munroe."

"That's funny. I have heard that name somewhere before…but maybe not. I'm not too sure. I sort of felt a touch of déjà vu when you said the name."

"Really? Maybe Detective Phil Duncan dropped the name by accident in the shop."

Bette sat down opposite her and ran her fingers through her fringe, "Yeah, that's probably it. Where else would I have heard it."

Chris finally showed up for his volunteer shift without a valid excuse, Raquel left to return to Proctor's warm embrace and Bette was left to ponder over that name. By then, the local townspeople had started to come in through the door to collect their parcels and she eventually forgot to remember it at all.

Chapter Sixteen

Raquel had only returned to her home once to bring back her makeup, some clothing, an extra pair of shoes and her toothbrush to Proctor's cottage.

They were enjoying their third day together as a couple with only a brief absence when Proctor had to ride into town to order the cherry picker and collect his mail. It was still far too hot to start work on the silos mural, so they spent time inside his cottage, keeping cool and finding time to watch television, movies, make love and collaborate on meal choices together. Once they went out riding together at sunset when it was getting cooler, Raquel on the borrowed bay mare. The McCarthys had very kindly agreed to loan Proctor the bay mare for a month. Raquel was starting to embrace her inner cowgirl and enjoyed wearing the Akubra hat and riding western style with her new man.

For a change in their routine, Raquel had been to the service station that morning and brought a couple of newspapers back to read.

Proctor was glued to the television when she walked in the front door. He was watching the summer tennis with a beer-can opened and a bowl of popcorn at his fingertips next to him on the couch. He was relaxing in his black silk bathrobe from Thailand, his long-tanned legs casually stretched out. The coffee table at his feet was covered in sketches for the mural. She thought he was starting to look like and act like a true Aussie male. She stared at him for a long minute, taking in his rugged facial features, his trim physique and thick grey hair. He certainly looked younger and fitter than his sixty-six years, but she did worry about their age difference at times.

They had already had a few minor disagreements. She loved Aussie rock music and played it loud. When Proctor entered the lounge room, he would turn it down. Or switch it off altogether and put on his favourite music which was Chopin, Vivaldi or Glen Campbell or Tom Jones at a medium level. He was also a roller of the toothpaste tube while she was a frustrated squeezer. He replaced the toilet roll and turned it under. When she replaced the toilet roll, the paper was positioned neatly over. He put the toilet lid neatly down while she raised it up. He was an enthusiastic early riser who bounced out of bed and did twenty sit-ups completely nude, while she put her mobile phone on snooze at least three times before she crawled out of bed and grumbled about the sun and made her blurry way to his coffee maker machine.

Another cause for concern was that he loved to watch old musicals and romantic films, while Raquel enjoyed reality TV and big action movies. But she overlooked his taste in musicals on the afternoon he held her tight against him in the loungeroom and twirled her around. He impressed her with his smooth rock and roll moves and he successfully danced her into his bedroom for another steamy sex session.

Proctor also preferred to cook and he was rather good at it too. He seemed to have the knack of putting various ingredients together and it just seemed to work. But when she made her famous chocolate mousse cheesecake, he didn't compliment her. But at least he was always respectful and his warm hugs were genuine.

"Hey. What you got there, my sweetheart?" He asked in his harsh whisper of a voice.

"Just some newspapers. Thought I'd catch up with the news and local gossip. I'm not crazy about watching sport."

He smiled up at her and put his right arm out to welcome her back onto the couch. But she waved her hand, dismissing his offer.

"No, it's alright. I'll go and read these at the dining table. Tennis is really not my thing, Phil."

He shrugged his shoulders and brushed his silver-grey hair back, "I can switch it off. I am just amazed at how much sport they show here on the free channels. I don't get this cricket stuff though. It's a really strange, slow game. I don't understand why people watch it."

She chuckled softly, "Yes. Very Aussie game, that one. Do you like our footy?"

"What the hell is that?"

"Okay. We'll watch when footy season starts. Way too hard to explain it right now. Well, I'll leave you to it."

She sat down at the dining table and studied the newspaper headlines first. It was all about the Brumby Flat murders. It seemed like the small town had suddenly become the epicentre of the world. She had moved into the town to enjoy some peace and quiet, and now, the whole world had somehow intruded upon it. The world had beat a path right to her door.

After a few minutes, she heard Proctor yell out from the lounge room, "What's in the news today?"

"It's all about Brumby Flat. The headline says 'Race to catch serial killer'. The other newspaper says 'Body exhumed and identified'. Oh, and I just read the death notices. Bridie Browne's funeral is on tomorrow. She was the postmistress, before Bette. Did you ever meet Bridie?"

Proctor cleared his throat and arched his back, "Oh okay. Yeah, I did. Just once. Went in to collect my mail. That's kind of sad."

"Yeah. It is. She had no family. Bette said."

"Oh, and I had a call from that city detective fella today too."

Raquel frowned and felt a shiver go down her spine, "What did he say to you?" she asked tersely. She hoped Duncan had not mentioned their brief liaison to Proctor.

"He just wanted to know if I would take on a new pet."

She stood up from her chair and walked over to lean against the loungeroom doorway.

"Did you say 'pet'? As in, a friendly animal that requires looking after and some feeding."

He nodded his head and finished off his beer in a gulp, "Yes, ma'am. Those were his exact words to me. He said he was looking for a home for a bluey? It's an Aussie dog breed, he said. The dog belonged to that old guy who died in that car accident last week. His daughter doesn't want to look after it, or his neighbours."

"And what did you say?"

"I hope it's not going to upset you, my sweet…but I said Okay. I'll take in the poor animal and give it a home. Might be a good guard dog for us. I kind of thought it might be a good idea since we got a killer still lurking around."

She sighed heavily, secretly relieved that Duncan had not rung up Phil Proctor to discuss her. He had obviously moved on and had some respect for her blossoming relationship with Proctor. Raquel knew it would not be easy being with Proctor. Because of his tall frame, his sexy American accent and man about town swagger, she knew he attracted the ladies like a cooked sausage attracts flies at an Aussie BBQ.

"Oh well, I think it's lovely of you to offer. I don't mind having a dog around the place. It's a type of cattle dog but I don't know if they do make good guard dogs. Guess we'll find out."

"The name's Max, short for Maxine. I think that's what he said. I get to pick her up tomorrow, in the afternoon."

"Phil, I think we should go to Bridie's funeral. Word around is that no one was really close to her. Bette called me at the service station. She said it will be a private gathering, but she has invited us personally. I think we should go."

Proctor pulled a face, "Hey, I am not too keen on funerals. However, if you really want to…sure, okay, I'll tag along, I guess. I might have to protect you anyway. I reckon there'll be a lot of media people around."

"I didn't think about that. I'd better make sure I look my best."

"I didn't bring over a suit from the States, but I can always wear my good jeans with a black jacket."

"Sounds good to me. And did you want to know the latest on Bridie's murder? The police believe she was viciously raped in the post office, and then apparently whoever it was bludgeoned her to death."

Proctor's face went ash white for a few seconds, "No, I didn't hear that story."

"It's in the papers if you want to read it. Her funeral's at half past ten tomorrow morning."

He got up and wrapped his bathrobe tighter around his waist, heading to the fridge to crack open another coldie.

"Sure thing. We'll go, if you want to," he replied, ripping open the beer top.

Hearing that Bridie was suspected of being raped and then murdered after, Proctor was starting to feel nervous. He secretly wondered if he was the last person to see her alive, the last to be with her before she was brutally murdered by someone else.

He watched Raquel walk across the lounge room in front of him. She stood at the window and peered through the lace curtains.

"Phil, I really feel like we are being watched," she stated, and she was right.

Proctor winked at her when she turned around, "I think you're letting your imagination run away with you. I'm here. Don't worry your pretty little head, my sweetheart."

****

Bette and Sandy Mitchell met Raquel and Proctor who were holding hands, inside the local funeral chapel. Outside, they had endured cameras in their faces, the media jostling to cover Bridie Browne's funeral. Specially hired security guards were keeping the media and the morbidly curious out.

The chapel was small, with just enough seating for fifty mourners. It was bright and white inside but felt small and cramped. The carpet was plush blue with a red *fleur de lis* pattern. At the foot of the altar, the elevated white coffin of Bridie loomed large, a large spray of elegant white lilies covering the casket lid.

Bette was dressed in a plain and simple Esprit black dress and silver strappy sandals. She completed her look with small cream gloves. Sandy looked uncomfortable in his only navy suit and large reflective sunglasses. Raquel was dressed in a black and white polka dot dress with a matching cap sleeve jacket. Proctor stood dutifully beside her, in his best Levi's and a smart black blazer. His fingers were threaded through hers and he occasionally squeezed her hand gently, reassuring her of his presence.

"What a circus," Bette sighed, looking briefly at her Sandy who was standing aloof and fidgeting.

Raquel smiled and playfully swung Proctor's arm, "It was scary. All those reporters. We didn't stop or say anything at all."

"We walked straight in. We were the same."

"Are we the only ones here?"

Bette shook her head, "No, I think the detectives are coming too. Surprised they aren't here already. It's a shame because I think we are it. Other people in town, well, they won't be sending her off today."

Sandy suddenly leaned in and whispered in his wife's ear.

"Okay. Well, I guess. Alright, see you later then."

Sandy inclined his head, said a quiet goodbye to all and left the chapel rather briskly.

"Sorry. My Sandy had to leave. Said he had a stomach ache. He told me this morning he wasn't feeling the best."

Raquel nodded, "Oh yeah. Sure. You didn't think you would make it here either," she said to Proctor, nudging his arm. He managed to smile very slightly.

"I reckon I'm better now."

"Well, it's not the best circumstances to meet again, doll."

The Manager of the funeral home suddenly appeared, in his sombre dark blue suit and introduced himself, shaking hands in turn.

"Are you all here to celebrate Bridie Browne's life?" he asked, straightening his tie and quickly assuming a pose of respect.

"Yes, we are," Bette replied softly.

"Are we family or friends of Bridie Browne?"

"Well. It's sort of complicated. But I took over her job and these are my friends, who knew her too. Not well. They sort of knew her. We're here to pay our respects."

At that moment, Detectives Duncan and Longmeil turned up, dressed in their best dark suits. Duncan stood tall and his intense blue eyes flashed over the small gathering, taking longer glances over Bette and Raquel.

"Well, a solemn day. Is anyone else here?" he asked.

Bette answered him, "No, just us three. My husband has just left. He has a stomach bug."

"I thought her uncle might turn up today. We did make contact with him a couple of times but he seems to be a very reserved fellow."

The Manager stepped forward, and introduced himself all over again to the detectives, shaking their hands in turn.

"Now, who is doing the eulogy today?"

The small group took turns, looking at each other searchingly.

Finally, Detective Duncan said, "I don't think anyone thought of it. She doesn't really have much in the way of family or friends. Maybe you can just give her a short blessing, a poem...or maybe a quote."

The Manager nodded, "I can just say a prayer to start with. And I could say some nice words about her."

Bette smiled, "That sounds perfect."

"So what was Bridie Browne like? What were her interests? I have to know a bit about her, to give her the truly lovely send-off she deserves."

There was a long uncomfortable silence, which was eventually broken by Bette's raspy voice, "I think she was an animal lover."

Raquel spoke up, "Yes, and she was a hard worker too. Spent lots of time in the Brumby Flat post office."

"I think she liked going to the pub too," Bette added.

Duncan snapped his fingers, "Ah yeah. Just remembered. Someone I interviewed recently said that Bridie liked the local football team."

Bette folded her arms and sniffed under her breath, "Why am I *not* surprised?"

"I seem to recall she had a real loving smile. A big welcoming smile."

Everyone turned around to look at Proctor who shrugged his shoulders, "Well, it's true. I noticed...ahh...she was real friendly when I went in...once...to collect some mail."

The funeral home manager nodded his head, "That's fantastic. Now I have an idea about her. Are you ready for us to start?"

"By all means, ladies first," Duncan gestured towards the open chapel doors.

They sat down in the front row. The manager did his very best with the small amount of information he had and talked for about five minutes. After he finished the eulogy, he played a quiet, respectful song in the background. One by one they stood up, filed past her closed coffin and placed a handful of rose petals on the lid. Bette and Raquel shed a few tears, while the men all looked uncomfortable. There was a sense of relief for them when the short service was over.

The manager gestured them to the tearoom next door.

"Help yourselves to tea, coffee and biscuits," he said with a gentle smile.

Bette was the first to speak after she had served herself a cup of filtered coffee,

"Who paid for the service? All this? It's really nice and respectful."

"The State arranged it. Until they sort out her estate, which may take some time. No Will," Duncan said, stirring his tea. He was trying hard not to notice Raquel and Proctor standing in the other corner of the room, still holding hands and talking quietly, their bodies pressed in against each other. He found he was still wrestling with his feelings for Raquel.

Detective Longmeil, who was unusually quiet, walked off to pour himself a filtered coffee and choose some biscuits. It offered Duncan and Bette the chance to talk alone for a few minutes.

"How's the investigations going, Detective Duncan?"

He smirked, "Not that well. Plus, I have to keep my eye on you. After this, where are you off to, Mrs Mitchell?"

"Home of course," she retorted swiftly, "to my husband."

"Okay. I'll follow you in my car."

"Oh good god, is that really necessary?"

He nodded and repositioned his slipping glasses back onto the bridge of his nose, "Just doing my job."

Suddenly, their full attention was diverted to the loving couple in the far corner of the room, who had raised their voices briefly. They saw Raquel lightly slap Proctor's left cheek. She then turned on her left heel and stormed off, straight out of the tearoom.

"Wow. What was that all about?" Duncan muttered.

"No idea. I didn't really hear their words," Bette replied, taking the last sip of her coffee.

"Must be very serious, she's definitely walked out."

Proctor stood still, hands thrust in his Levi's pockets. He was looking down at the carpet, seeming to reflect on the recent event of his lover's abrupt departure. He then turned his head and with a pained expression on his ruggedly handsome face, he clearly mouthed the word 'sorry' to Bette and nodded to Duncan and followed suit. Detective Longmeil took the opportunity to take some more biscuits while no one was looking.

Proctor caught up with Raquel in the carpark as she prepared to drive away angry. She had already started up her car and looked up at him, as he leaned down, elbows resting on her open car window.

"Hey, where are you going?" he asked.

"Home, back to my own home. Thank you very much."

"Wait, whoa, honey. Let's talk."

She raised her voice, tears streaming down her face, "I am not your bloody black horse. There's nothing more to say, Phil. I am so disappointed with you. I can't believe…you didn't tell me the truth. You tell me now at her bloody funeral."

"No, no. She meant nothing to me," he lowered his voice, looking out for the media, "I wasn't with you when it happened. I didn't really know you then. I care about only you, my sweetheart. What I'm feeling for you, believe me, is entirely different than being with Bridie."

She shook her head, "I'm sorry Phil, but I'm truly upset for a few reasons. I have to leave now."

"I'm not her killer. Please, my sweetheart. Believe me. Don't go. Don't go off like this."

"You had sex with her and for all I know, you killed her too."

She averted her eyes from him and put her car into a hard reverse. Proctor was forced to lift his arms away and step right back. He watched her car disappear through the gates and down the hill, back to town.

As she drove through the funeral home gates, Raquel had a quick glance in her rear vision mirror. She saw Proctor get ambushed by a rogue group of reporters.

Raquel went home to her place, she watched the evening news and saw the footage from the outside of the funeral home, including a glimpse of Proctor, ducking, weaving and putting his hand up at the camera. She cried herself to sleep that evening. She was upset because Phil Proctor had not confided in her earlier and entrusted her with details of his secret liaison with Bridie. If what he had told her was all true, she realised that he may have been the last person to see the post office mistress alive.

Chapter Seventeen

After two days at home, Raquel was climbing the walls. She found that she missed Phil Proctor more than she had anticipated she would.

Whatever she picked up or looked at, seemed to remind her of Proctor. Her round hairbrush made her think of his cock, when she saw her toothpaste, she thought of being in his bathroom and sharing the shower with him and whenever she held a dinner fork in her hand, she thought instantly of Bridie Browne. She missed his voice, his easy smile and just being near his charismatic presence which always thrilled and excited her.

Proctor had tried to call her mobile, but she let all his calls go to her messages, and eventually, she blocked him altogether.

She was sitting in her large kitchen, still surrounded by a tower of unpacked boxes, thinking about the funeral and reliving Proctor's words of confession. Her cup of instant coffee had turned cold by the time she remembered she had made herself one. She realised that she needed to get out of the house for a while, and she thought of her friend Bette. She made the snap decision to go and see her, and confide her fears about Proctor. Was he the Brumby Flat serial killer?

She expected to find Bette at the shop but there was no answer to her frantic knocking. She then drove her trusty Firebird to Bette's home on the edge of town. There were only two places to find Bette.

She walked around the side of the house, expecting to find her friend curled up in her cabana, sipping a cocktail. But it was strangely empty, with only solar lamps twinkling away and around her in the surrounding garden beds. She could see in the distance that the tennis court lights were off, so she knew Bette was not there either.

She shrugged her shoulders and went to the backdoor which led into Bette's very grand blackwood and granite benchtop kitchen. As she neared the flyscreen door, she heard voices talking in hushed whispers inside. Raquel stopped her walking and held her breath for a few moments. She wanted to know who it was and overhear what they were saying. Bette had told her that everyone staying at her B&B was secretive. She knew it was wrong to eavesdrop but she was tired of missing secrets, like the Bridie bombshell Proctor had set off.

She stepped closer very quietly, and through the side of the flyscreen door, she could make out two people walking around the kitchen. She finally recognised Bette as one of them. Bette was in her bikini, wearing a see-through sequin kaftan over it. She was smiling broadly and her bright blue eyes were dancing. She was whispering animatedly but Raquel could not make out what she was saying. She was clearly talking to someone else.

Just then the mysterious other person appeared from the opposite corner of the room. It was Detective Duncan, smirking at Bette's quiet words to him and enthusiastically nodding his head. Raquel stepped away from the doorway and gasped. She had seen how close they were standing next to each other. She was almost certain she had seen Duncan bend over and kiss Bette's lips briefly, but her view was obstructed, and she reasoned to herself that shadows can be deceiving.

Raquel stepped back a bit more and decided to make her entrance just that little bit louder for them.

She took a deep breath, straightened her navy dress and then yelled out, "Hello? Is anyone home? Bette? hello?"

A chirpy reply echoed back, "Come in, come in."

Raquel opened the squeaky screen door and just as she expected to find them, Bette and Detective Duncan were now positioned at opposite ends of her vast kitchen.

"Hey doll," Bette smiled at her sympathetically while Duncan just inclined his head in a vague acknowledgement. "How are you? How are you feeling? You looked really upset at the funeral."

"I'm alright. I didn't mean to run out the way I did. I'm sorry about that."

Bette reached out and gently took Raquel's right hand into her own, "That's okay. I am just happy to see you. I have been wondering how you were."

Raquel knitted her eyebrows, thinking if Bette had been really concerned, she would have called her.

"Well, Proctor and I, we just had a bit of a misunderstanding."

"Oh, dear. That's no good. Have you both sorted things out now?"

Raquel shook her head, "No. Not exactly. I am thinking…I will go and see him. Put everything on the table."

She really wanted to talk to Bette alone, but Duncan stood firm. He was leaning casually against the pantry cupboard, wiping his smudged glasses with a tissue, which just seemed to increase the width of the smudges.

"Fair enough, doll. Sometimes we all need to take a breather away from our partners. You know, to have time to work things through. Relationships are not the easiest thing."

"True, true," Detective Duncan chimed in, giving his two cents worth.

"If you care about Proctor still, you have to give him space, which you have. And then, you reach out to him when you are ready."

"Yes, I miss him but we both need to discuss a few issues."

Bette smiled, tight-lipped, "Do you want to talk about it, doll?" she asked.

Raquel flicked her eyes to the floor and managed a quick sideways glance at Detective Duncan under her eyelashes. She decided it was better not to attract Duncan's interest in Phil Proctor with a mention of his brief liaison with Bridie in the post office.

"It's fine, really. I will sort it out, on my own. It's just personal stuff, you know."

"Okay, doll. I understand."

"Oh, how is Anabella doing? Is she still…"

Duncan quickly cut in, "Yeah, well, Mrs Williams seems to be doing okay. She's in a secure women's prison but it's very relaxed. She is cooperating with the police, through her lawyer. Can't say too much, but you never know. Things may go in her favour."

He went on to suggest they should visit her one day soon, but no one said a word in reply.

Suddenly, a loud bell sounded and Bette sprang into action.

"Excuse me, one of the guests must have a bit of a problem or some sort of query. I'll be back as soon as I can."

Raquel was left in the kitchen, blinking up at Detective Duncan under the harsh fluorescent lights. She folded her arms and stepped closer to him, speaking in a hushed tone,

"What the hell are you doing? Are you messing around with my best friend? And you know exactly what I mean."

He pulled a face, "Are we in a relationship? Am I answerable to you?" he whispered back in his angry, annoyed voice.

"No but she's my best friend and I care very much about her. And what was that kiss about?"

His jaw dropped, "What the…? You were spying on us outside?" he exclaimed.

"Suddenly, I am not available and you move straight in, on my good friend,"

"Hey, hey. Don't assume that you know me that well. In fact, not that long ago, you said you hated me. I didn't kiss Bette, okay? I know she's a married woman but I do need to keep an eye on her. I am sure that the killer may come looking for her. I am here, trying to protect her actually."

She shook her head, "You're unbelievable, Phil Duncan. Playing that card on me. You're playing with bloody fire. But okay, whatever. Anyway, I'm going. I don't want to know any more about it."

She turned around and continued her rant at him, "You know, I wouldn't be shocked if you came out here and killed these people, just to get to know me. You knew I lived in Brumby Flat."

Detective Duncan laughed heartily, "Who's the crazy person here? I can't believe where your crazy imaginings are taking you."

Raquel turned back to leave.

"Where are you going?" he followed her to the backdoor.

"Home."

"To Phil Proctor's?" he smirked, his tone making her turn sharply around.

"It really is none of your business."

"Good. Then you keep out of mine."

She glared at him for a second longer and then slammed the screen door soundly shut, as she left.

****

The next morning, Raquel walked out onto her front veranda, clutching her cup of instant coffee. She had woken up with a brand-new vision of the world. Deep down, she had searched her soul and realised that Phil Proctor was very possibly her one true love. She didn't want to lose him now, and even the Bridie Brown revelation was not enough to dissuade her from loving him.

In the distance, on the hill above the town, she could see a tall, elegant figure on a black horse, and a dog circling. She was sure it was Proctor and it seemed to her that he was getting on with his life without her. She leaned against the railing post, tears welling in the corners of her eyes but she quickly wiped them away. She gulped her coffee down and retreated inside. She had finally unblocked him on her phone but he had not tried to call her anymore.

For the next two hours, she madly cleaned her kitchen and lounge room, unpacked a couple of moving boxes and grappled with her conscience. She had to talk herself into giving Proctor another chance. She finally made the decision to walk up to his cottage on the hill and chat with him. She needed a good long walk to clear her head anyway. Work had called her in, but she told them quite firmly she was in the middle of a mental health day.

It was another really hot day outside, so she grabbed a bottle of ice-cold water from her fridge on her way out the front door,

She had her flat black shoes on too, but she could still feel the pebbles and stones on the footpath as she briskly started her walk.

She had only taken about fifty steps, when an old pickup truck, possibly from the nineteen-forties came flying down the main street, raising a plume of red dust from the bitumen. The paintwork had mostly peeled away, leaving it a patchy brown and a rusty red in parts. It came to a jerky, rattly stop in front of her, just an inch away from the kerb. She had no idea who it belonged to. The drivers' door suddenly swung wide open, with a loud creaky squeak. And there was Phil Proctor, smiling point-blank at her. He jumped down from the cabin.

She shaded her eyes from the sun and looked at him puzzled. She took one very hesitant step towards the truck.

"Hello. What's this?" she said.

"I bought her over today because I've fixed her up. Took me a few days. But she runs really well now."

"What do you want, Phil?" she asked him, keeping her voice ice-cool, calm and collected.

He decided to turn on all his manly charm, brushing his right hand through his mane of silver-grey hair. She did notice his loose white linen shirt with his tight Levi's jeans and the lingering women's perfume he liked to wear. He leaned in towards her and put on his best winsome smile.

"Well, it's a pickup truck and I thought…I might just pick you up, ma'am. Why? Did you have some other plans today?"

Raquel shook her head, "No. Okay, I was just coming up to see you."

"I'm right here. Come on. Let's take her for a long country drive. How about it, sweetheart?"

She looked at him and then walked over to the other side of the truck. She opened the creaky passenger door to climb up into the seat which was a cracked black vinyl and rock hard to boot. She had to hitch up her skirt to get up into the cabin. They slammed their respective doors shut and Proctor turned the key over. The engine splattered under the bonnet and shook the truck back into life.

"Where are we going?" she asked him.

He winked at her and then reversed the truck with it's one good mirror, "I'd like to chance it. A long run on the open freeway would be great. Got a full tank of gas."

The truck was noisy and Raquel had to adjust her voice to make herself heard above the splattering and shuddering sounds.

"I was coming to see you. I wanted to tell you that I was sorry."

He nodded and kept his eyes on the road as he drove them straight out of town, "I know, my sweetheart. Believe me, I am sorry too."

"Yeah, I needed some time to think about you and me. I realised…well, I think I already knew you are not the serial killer. I have to be honest with you. I was very shocked that you and Bridie had got it together," she studied her hands in her lap and then realised she still had the bottle of water. She placed it under the seat for later.

He put his warm left hand gently but firmly on her thigh and skirt, "It's okay. I understand. I get it. But it was one time only. Anyway, it was before we even got together. I've missed you. And I don't care about the damn past. Just leave it there, sweetheart, in the past."

"Yeah, you're right."

"Hey there. How about we go to the rodeo this weekend? And I reckon I read something about the Brumby Flat Cup being on and the Lithuanian javelin throwing team will be there too. Don't know how this is going to play out on the oval, but it might be good fun."

He wound the drivers' side window right down, and Raquel smiled up at him, and she did the same. The warm breeze picked up her shoulder-length blonde hair and lightly teased it. They headed down the open two-lane country road, and there was silence for a good five minutes, with just the growling sound of the engine and the whistling of the wind. The truck had only a top speed of sixty-five kilometres flat out, so the dry, red, dusty countryside slipped by in a kind of slow motion.

"Phil."

"Yes, ma'am," he changed gears on the column shift.

"I really want to make it up to you. I feel like a bit of excitement, you know?"

He grinned and glanced at her sideways for a moment, mindful of keeping his eyes on the road ahead, "Do you want me to pull over now?" he asked her in a harsh whisper, "We're in the middle of nowhere."

"No. I hope you're a really good driver. You'll have to concentrate hard and hold that wheel tight."

Proctor knitted his eyebrows together and wondered what game she was playing at.

"Hey, girlie, I have been driving for forty-five years. I can drive anything you throw at me. I reckon I can cope with any situation on the road too. It feels really good to be driving again, but strange being on the other side of the road."

She removed her seatbelt and replied, "This is dangerous and so very, very wrong."

He raised his eyebrows as she moved closer to him, sliding across the bench seat and then she bent her head down into his lap. He rolled his tongue over his top lip as she proceeded to undo the zip of his tight blue jeans. He could feel the blood rushing and pulsing through his cock and it was close to rock hard by the time Raquel enveloped it into her warm mouth.

"Oh sweet Jesus, girlie," he said in a gasp. His grip on the steering wheel tightened and he knew he would really have to hold it together.

She expertly used her right hand and lips in a rhythmic way to bring him to the inevitable climax. She gently, expertly teased his cock with her lips and probing tongue. His breathing became gradually faster and his foot was easing off and then pressing the accelerator as his pleasure kept building. She gradually increased her pace.

As they continued their sexy country drive, two road trains, a motorcyclist and a row of classic cars overtook and roared past them. Neither of them was particularly concerned if anyone could see what they were doing. For Proctor, it was a deliciously new sexual experience in a good lifetime full of them.

Proctor's breathing gradually increased, and he could feel the intense euphoria building within. When he finally exploded his cum into her warm mouth, he moaned deep within his throat and the truck bunny hopped down the road for about a hundred metres. Fortunately, no other cars were in sight or on the road at the time. He finally took better control of the truck, as Raquel sat back in the passenger seat and licked her moist lips. She clipped on the seatbelt quietly and calmly and sunk her head back into the cracked vinyl upholstery. His jeans were still unzipped but he didn't mind that at all.

Proctor expertly changed gears and slowed the pickup truck to a comfortable speed of sixty kilometres.

His eyes glazed over, thinking how wonderful that blow job was. He rested his warm left hand on her knee. In response, she lightly squeezed her hand over his.

"Are we all good now?" he half-whispered to her.

"Phil. If it's alright with you, I don't want to spend another day here on earth without you."

"Done. Move back in tonight."

She nodded her head.

"Shit, Raquel. We are a perfect fit, you know that?"

He glanced at her for a moment, flashing a quick smile. Then with his left hand, he lifted her skirt up a couple of inches. He slowly ran his hand up her bare inside thigh, his fingers seeking out her panties, and instead, finding her wet pussy.

Raquel relaxed, licked her lips and parted her legs. She had no intention of playing hard to get. He kept right on driving, pleasuring her with his fingers as he kept his eyes focused on the open stretch of road ahead.

Along the way to her screaming climax, three road trains rolled past, and a large flock of wayward emus galloped along the opposite side of the road, in their usual chaotic, nonsensical manner.

****

While Proctor and Raquel were enjoying their ride of intimacy down the highway, Detective Duncan was busy doing some research at the local police station. He had plugged his laptop in at Constable Banner's neat and efficient desk. He had a few leads now, which he wanted to check in the criminal database. But Constable Banner was hovering around him, his interest in investigative work sparked by the town murders.

"Do you need any more help?"

Duncan shook his head, "I'm right. All connected."

"How long will you be?"

Duncan shrugged his shoulders, "No idea."

"And is it true about what I heard?"

Duncan spun his chair around, "What have you heard?"

Constable Banner casually leant back on the edge of the desk and then positioned himself on the corner, "Don't you know? You've got the whole town talking. You've found love in town, they're all saying."

"I have? Oh, I have," he smirked, "Who am I with?"

Banner shook his head and smiled back, the skin around his eyes crinkled, "That new lady in town. Willaston, is it? Mate, I thought she was with the other Phil, that American guy who's old enough to be her father. But half the town says you're the one she's actually with. Is that true?"

"Hey, look, Constable. I have to be honest, but I have had to push back. It's not the thing, to put a relationship in the spotlight, in a town with a serial killer on the loose. So if you can keep a lid on it, much appreciated. A relationship is not something I should be concentrating on right now."

"Right, right. You let her go? Wow, fuck. That's noble of you. That old silver fox seems to be the ladies man."

Duncan smirked, "It's okay. I'll be leaving this town as soon as I can, so I am not interested in pursuing any kind of relationship."

Banner nodded enthusiastically, "Yeah, I thought you would be a sensible guy. You must know what small towns like this can be like. They are tough places to live in. Reputations can be destroyed by a few well-chosen words."

"It's okay. You are telling me it's best to keep our noses clean. I understand, more than you know."

Banner jumped off the desk corner and moved towards the front door, his hands characteristically resting on his hips, "I'd better go and leave you to your work."

Duncan was relieved when Banner disappeared, as much as he was disappointed that Detective Longmeil wasn't available that weekend, to help him work on the case. But then, he didn't have a clue about Longmeil's problems at home. His wife Laura was threatening to leave him with the kids, because she was sick of preparing his vegan meals separately to the kids' serve of chops and curried sausages, his many days away on his investigation work and his obsession with his cycling. The bicycle took up a lot of room propped up in their narrow hallway.

Duncan restlessly fiddled with and furiously tapped his pen against the desk. He was relieved that the body in the grave had been formally identified. He was eighteen-year-old Tom Munroe who actually died in the car accident, which happened just outside Brumby Flat thirty-two years ago. The most likely scenario was that Tom had stolen one of the Burfords' cars, which he had then rolled on an isolated dirt road. More than likely, Christopher Burford might have given chase and came across the tragic accident scene. He then had very conveniently switched identities, supposedly dying at the steering wheel of his own Ford Falcon XY. Duncan frowned at the thought of the deception and was sure he had reconstructed the right story. It was all over the newspapers, radio and the internet now.

After some research, Detective Duncan had turned up evidence that Burford had been living up and down the New South Wales coast, posing as Tom Munroe. Munroe's family said that Tom had disappeared at the time of the car accident, although from time to time, reports came back to them about him but the descriptions never quite matched their own recollections of Tom. And what he did was quite out of character for their Tom.

Burford had obviously carried around Munroe's IDs and wallet with him, but when his body was found at the base of the silos, there was no wallet on him or any form of ID. Detective Duncan assumed that someone, probably his killer, had claimed these and conveniently disposed of them. The killer was obviously very keen to keep a lid on this thirty-two-year-old secret but the net was starting to close in around them.

Duncan glanced over his suspect list and made his usual clicking sound with his tongue. He hoped he could be confident of the identity of the Brumby Flat killer by weekend's finish. That was his only plan before murder number four could potentially happen. He knew he had to stop the killing once and for all in Brumby Flat. Maybe then, he could finally go back home to Adelaide. He really wanted to put some distance between him and Bette, and Raquel as well. He had not planned to start developing feelings for a married woman, who was also a leading suspect in the murder investigations. It played on his mind quite a bit. He really didn't know what to do or what to expect next.

Suddenly, his mobile ringtone broke the silence. He looked at the screen, hesitated as he knew who it was but still, he answered it.

"Hi, Mrs Bette Mitchell."

"Hello, how are you?"

"In the office, working away. Where are you?"

"At home. Sandy's still away. He rang me just then, saying he's unloading a rig in Broken Hill. Then loading up again for a Coober Pedy run."

"Sounds like you'll be alone for a couple of days," he took a sharp intake of breath before continuing, "Can I ask you, who does Sandy work for?"

"I don't ask questions. I know there's a couple of freight places he works for locally. He always keeps busy, you know. He loves being on the road, he tells me. Why? Is he a murder suspect?"

"Everyone in this town is. Except we can rule out Mrs Williams and everyone who's already dead."

Bette went silent for a moment, "Well, I'll leave you to your important work then."

Final Chapter, or Is It?

Proctor and Raquel were casually walking arm in arm down the main street of Brumby Flat after going to the rodeo in the next town. Proctor had bought them a beer each and treated her to a hotdog with the lot. When she couldn't see the action, he calmly lifted her up and placed her on a high stone step in the grandstand, so she had a great, uninterrupted view.

As they walked along the main street, they both noticed that it was starting to get unusually dark very quickly. A giant mass of dark grey clouds hovered above. Raquel stopped and thought she could hear the rumble of lightning in the distance.

"Can you feel it?" she exclaimed, "Oh my God. It's rain. I feel the rain."

Raquel put the palm of her hand out and squealed with delight to Proctor. The raindrops were large splashy ones and eventually, the heavens opened up. A torrent of water rained down on them. Raquel joyously lifted her arms above her head and then smoothed her blonde hair back as if she were having a shower by herself.

Proctor stood in the warm rain, watching her and was quietly enjoying every second of it. She was a woman turned into a girl. Her T-shirt top clung tantalisingly to her pale skin. Her bra and her tan stretch trousers acted like a second skin.

His western check shirt too, started to cling to him in parts, though his head was semi-protected by his wide Akubra hat. His jeans were being splashed on but had some protection afforded by his authentic Texan cowboy boots.

She started to twirl around in the rain and smiled at him broadly, water caressing her eyelids, her cheeks, her lips and her curves.

"Young lady, you're making my head spin," he said in his half-whisper of a voice.

She stepped forward and he did the same. Standing within an inch of his grasp, he roped her against him with his strong arms, her wet body and clothes clinging to him quite deliciously. The rain dripped off the edges of his Akubra hat onto her shoulders as he enveloped her lips in a hot, steamy, lingering kiss.

"Hey, get a room!" they heard someone shout out to them.

They turned around and saw that they were no longer alone in the main street. A crowd of local residents had appeared out of their homes and were also rejoicing in the return of the rain. It heralded the end of a long two-year drought.

The couple laughed and still clung to each other as if they were afraid to let the moment go.

"You're crazy, but I'm crazy mad about you," Proctor said, one arm still locked around the small of her back and the fingers of her right hand locked in his other hand. He held her hand up and kissed it.

He whispered in her ear, "I would fuck you slowly in the rain, if the damn town wasn't all out here, watching us."

She smiled up at him.

"Tomorrow I have to really start painting the silos. Well, if this rain lets up. I'm gonna miss you, girlie. But I'll try and be home before dark."

She looked like she was crying but it was hard for him to tell, because of the monsoonal like rainfall.

"I know. I understand. Anyway, I'd better go home and change out of these wet clothes. Bette wanted to see me in the shop before I start my shift in the morning. I'm working on my own tomorrow."

"Okay, my sweetheart."

He gave her a light peck on her full lips and very reluctantly let her go.

Raquel had a quick shower and blow-dried her hair. She put a light foundation on her face. She changed into a lightweight, fitted linen dress but added a faux fur-trimmed parka. The temperature outside had finally dropped dramatically and it was still raining quite hard. On the television, the news had said three months' worth of rain would hit the region over the next twenty-four hours. She hoped the drought wasn't giving way to a flood situation.

She left her house and under the cover of the front veranda, she walked to the shop. It was a hard-driving rainstorm outside. She rapped loudly on the shop window. It was dark inside, but she could see a glimmer of light at the very back of the shop. She rapped on the window again, this time much louder.

Finally, she saw the back door open and Bette came out, looking immaculate in a new shiny black satin suit. She fiddled with the shop lock. As Raquel entered, Bette bent down to scoop up some pieces of paper from the floor. She studied them for a few seconds and said, "Oh wow, look, Orders for umbrellas and rain jackets," out aloud.

"I'm glad you're here, doll. I thought Proctor had dashed you off for the night," Bette remarked with a wry smile and her vivid blue jay eyes fluttered.

"I think he wanted to," Raquel sighed deeply, "Isn't it wonderful, all this rain finally."

"It's like a monsoon has hit us. Now doll. I'm going to be flat out with postal duties. Coming up to Christmas, I am expecting over three thousand parcels in the next week."

"Right. You need me to know how to use that coffee machine in a more efficient manner."

"Well, yes. But I also wanted to show you where we hide the shop float and the spare keys. This way."

Bette walked in front and as they entered the back room, they heard an audible beep from her jacket top pocket.

"Hang on, doll. Just a minute," she muttered, reading her mobile screen and then tapping her quick reply, "Just responding to Detective Duncan."

"Oh, okay. What does he want?"

"Well, it's the latest thing he's hot about. Wants to know where I am, all the bloody time. Oh yeah, and I needed to show this too."

Bette patted her hand around under the back counter and finally produced a couple of glossy postcards.

"Our army guy Chris had these made up, to sell here, in the shop."

Raquel studied the images closely. There was a jumbled collage of the silos and the post office building with police crime scene tape around them, accompanied with the words

'Welcome to Brumby Flat, murder capital of Australia' written in blood-red Halloween style lettering.

"Oh, dear. It's a bit confronting," Raquel said, putting them down on the countertop.

"Yes, I don't think we should sell these here. Oh. And I had to tell you that I have ordered some new stock this morning. People will be thinking of pools and swimming this summer, so I've ordered a range of floaties, flippers, masks and snorkels."

Suddenly, they heard a loud smashing sound. Actually, it was a sequence of them coming from the front of the shop. Bette and Raquel looked at each other searchingly.

"What was that?" Raquel lowered her voice.

Bette shrugged her shoulders and touched her index finger to her lips. They crouched down quietly against the backroom door. They heard footsteps, like heavy boots, walking around in the front room. They echoed on the timber floor and crunched down on broken shards of glass.

"Oh my god. Someone's broken in, through the window," Raquel whispered in Bette's ear.

Then a second later, a familiar voice sliced the eerie silence, "Honey bunch, are you in there?"

Bette sighed in relief and smiled, "It's okay. It's just my Sandy."

"Yes, my love, I'm right here," she yelled out and got up smiling, but Raquel stayed right where she was, half-hidden in the shadows. She was still feeling edgy from the sound of breaking glass. She wasn't feeling that safe and wished Phil Proctor was still around.

Sandy burst into the back room, brandishing an iron bar in his gloved right hand. He had a very serious expression on his tanned face. One that Bette could not read. He was dripping wet from the rainstorm outside, standing in a puddle of his own making. Fortunately, he did not see Raquel who was crouched behind the door he had just burst his way through.

Bette took an awkward step backwards and widened her eyes.

"What's wrong, love? Did you chase a burglar away? I heard glass smashing."

"You," he snapped back, his eyes narrowing, "That's what's fuckin' wrong."

"What?"

"Yeah, Bette, you heard me. I've had enough of you and this fuckin' shop. You're never home much anymore. This isn't a marriage. I've bent over backwards for you, you ungrateful little bitch."

He adjusted his grip on the iron bar.

"Sandy honey, we can talk things over."

"I have suffered with you for the last twenty years. I don't love you. There's no point us going on."

"What do you mean, honey?"

"I mean exactly that, I never loved you. And I hate this bloody shithole of a town too."

A strange realisation entered Bette's mind, "My god. Did you kill all those people? Sandy…" she cried.

"Did you think we came to live here, in Brumby bloody Flat by luck?"

"Oh my god."

"Yep. You may as well know the truth. I knew all about Chris Burford and his identity switch. I helped with the cover-up over thirty years ago, you know. And Bridie Browne, you might as well know about us too."

"Sandy, what's going on?"

"Bette, we were having an affair. I only killed Bridie because she was a stupid, dumb slut. Couldn't keep her bloody fuckin' legs shut, could she? She told me that she loved me, and then she started screwing some guy behind my back. I even heard them fuckin' like rabbits in the post office."

"Oh, dear God," tears started to stream down her cheeks.

"I saw Chris arrive back here in Brumby Flat. I had to try to keep the secret. You saw him arrive too, I know you did. I saw you from across the street. But I never planned to kill you, my dear wife. I was planning to leave town with Bridie, but shit happens I suppose. She had no intention of changing her ways for me."

He took a deep breath and then continued.

"And yeah, I killed that farmer. I saw the old 'cocky' drive him into town and he had to go too. I made that one look like it was a car accident. That was easy."

Sandy stepped forward, his murderous intent shining in his black eyes. Raquel tried to shrink further into the dark shadows. Bette stepped back again and looked fearfully side to side, frantically looking for a way to escape.

"Sandy, you don't have to do this. I can keep my mouth shut. Honestly, I can. No one needs to know about any of this. You could leave town tonight and I won't say a word about what you just said to me. I promise I won't tell a soul."

He lunged forward and grabbed her left wrist. He twisted it sharply.

"Sandy. You're hurting me," she cried out.

"Good. See how it feels to be helpless? I am finally in control of you," he sneered, "I made you bloody cocktails, listened to your silly little shop talk. La-de-da-da. Set up your spa, your sauna and put up with your expensive crappy taste all these years. After you're gone, I'm off, my dear wife."

Raquel leapt out of the shadows and shoved him hard from behind. He lost his grip of Bette's wrist out of surprise and she managed to leap out of his way when he tried to grab at her again. Annoyed, he turned and swung the iron bar at Raquel who skilfully dodged it, thanks to her old but well remembered acrobatic skills. Bette dodged behind Sandy and together Bette and Raquel raced into the front of the shop which was completely dark, except for the light of the streetlamp streaming inside. Raquel grabbed Bette's sweaty, shaking right hand and said, "Go. Front door." They crab-stepped around the large merchandise tables.

But Sandy was already positioned there, the iron bar raised up in his right fist. The women stepped back again, trying to work out which way to jump next.

"We're going to die," Bette cried out and then she started to scream.

"Shut up, no, we won't! Run," Raquel forcibly turned her friend in a different direction.

At that precise moment, Phil Proctor raced in, leaping through the broken glass window and wordlessly, he lunged forward and tackled Sandy Mitchell to the floor. Out of shock, Sandy had dropped the iron bar which connected with the timber floor. It fell with a loud thud.

Raquel and Bette clung to each other. It was too dark for them to see who had the upper hand.

There were arms and legs flailing in the air. Punches were raining down. Proctor, however, knew what his position was. He was not a young man anymore, but he was clever and conservative with his movements and actions. He was taller than his adversary. He also had strong muscular arms which ably deflected Sandy's rain of fist blows.

Proctor had managed to push away the iron bar under one of the shop's merchandise tables, well away from Sandy's reach. He was using his torso and strong arms as a barrier to Sandy grabbing a hold of it again. But the distraction cost Proctor dearly. He was so busy deflecting blows that he didn't see Sandy pull out a knife from underneath his jacket.

Sandy cursed Proctor loudly under his breath, and then struck hard. The knife connected into the side of Proctor's abdomen. It went in two inches. Proctor winced and pulled away, the blade still stuck firmly in his left side. Raquel saw the knife protruding there and screamed. Proctor sunk to his knees, clutching his injured side.

Sandy regained his feet and looked ready to kill, "You're an interfering little bitch," he sneered at Raquel, "You slut. You brought him into it. Fuck. I have to kill the fuckin' lot of you now."

With Proctor now winded and clutching his side, Sandy went to grab the iron bar which was under a table. Proctor saw him move for it and struggled to stand, determined to stop him. But he fell back onto his knees.

Suddenly, another shadow appeared, stepping over the broken shop window, with a handgun raised ominously. A glint of light from the streetlamp revealed his identity. It was Senior Detective Phillip Duncan whose brown pinstripe suit was half drenched by the deluge of monsoonal rain. His white shirt was stuck damp against his chest. His eyes quickly adjusted to the dim lighting and he saw who he needed to see.

"Stop. Stand up where you are," Detective Duncan barked in his commanding voice, his gun aimed squarely at Sandy's heaving chest, "Don't you dare move, Mitchell. Keep your hands up where I can see them."

Sandy froze but his murderous mind looked to be still working away.

"Fuck you," he said under his breath.

"Proctor's hurt," Raquel cried out from the far corner.

"Okay, you see to Proctor."

Raquel ran around the other side of the table to Proctor's side and kneeled beside him. He had heaved himself to sit upright against a shop wall, "Oh my god, Phil. You're bleeding."

His white T-shirt entertained a small but spreading red stain around the knife blade lodged above his hip.

He half-smiled up at her and winked, "Yes, ma'am, making a bit of a mess here. Hurts like hell but…okay. I reckon I'm okay."

Duncan barked out more instructions, "Find some material and compress it on his wound. Leave the knife where it is. How badly hurt are you, Proctor?"

"I reckon I'll live, detective. It went through my side. I reckon it's missed anything vital. I'm not bleeding too much, so don't worry about me. Keep your eye on that crazy son of a bitch over there."

"Bette, here, use my mobile to call an ambulance," Raquel threw it to Bette who caught it easily.

"Down on your knees," Duncan shouted at Sandy who very slowly obliged him.

"Turn to your left slowly. Now put your hands behind you," Duncan stepped forward and quickly cuffed his wrists behind his back and then pushed him face-first down onto the floor. His gun was still raised, "Sandy Mitchell. You're under arrest on suspicion of several murders. And now attempted murder. Or attempted murders. Anyway, there's a string of other charges still to come." He quickly read him his rights.

In the meantime, Raquel had torn off a tattered ribbon of an old white tablecloth and pressed it against Proctor's wounded left side. He flinched at her firm touch and welcomed it at the same time.

"Don't die on me, Phil Proctor. You have Silos to finish painting. I want to go riding with you, and see lots more sunsets."

His fingertips gently touched her face, especially wiping a solitary tear from her cheek, "My sweetheart, I couldn't leave you if I tried. I'm okay, really."

Duncan watched the pair of them out of the corner of his eye. He felt a bit jealous, but he could see the genuine spark of love in her eyes for Proctor. It was something he secretly wished for too.

Bette returned from whispering away on the mobile, wiping away her tears of fear and frustration, having learnt the shocking truth about her husband, "The ambulance is on its way. So are the police. They said about twenty minutes."

"Phil, thank you," Raquel lovingly kissed Proctor's forehead.

"Sweetheart, something told me to come back. I went to your house but you didn't answer. I came up to the shop and saw the broken glass. I wanted to see you again, you see. I'd do it all again for you. No hesitation. I am so happy that you are okay," he half-whispered.

He gently placed his arm around her and she did the same but very carefully, as they waited patiently for the ambulance to arrive. She kept pressure on around his wound. They listened to the rain still falling heavily outside.

Duncan piped up, his gun still trained on Sandy, "I ran a check tonight on your husband, Mrs Mitchell. There was a connection to Christopher Burford which came up. That's why I'm here. And lucky I made it here in time too."

They all nodded. No one was going to argue with him while he was holding a gun.

"They were good mates in high school. As near as I can figure out, Chris wanted a way out of this town. He didn't get along with his father. When this young guy called Tom Munroe was killed in a car accident, I believe they both appeared at the accident. scene Chris switched identities. He had been living up and down the New South Wales coast posing as Tom Munroe."

Bette stepped forward and asked, "I don't understand? How did they get away with that, for so long?"

Duncan smirked, "With your Sandy's help, of course, Mrs Mitchell. But one day, Sandy stopped sending money to help keep him out of trouble. Chris had become something of a burden to Sandy who turned his back on him. Chris ended up struggling and homeless. How am I doing so far, Sandy?"

Sandy grunted, "I need a lawyer."

Duncan smirked and replied, "Of course, you do. You were just damn lucky thirty-two years ago. No one really asked the right questions. It appears that Chris and Tom were similar in both height and build. It was easy for Chris Burford to leave town as Tom, while poor Tom went underground. We just raised him up from a very long sleep. Sandy eventually left town too. But you should tell your wife what your real name used to be, Sandy. Before you had it changed legally."

"No way I'm saying anything. I'll wait for my lawyer, thank you."

Duncan continued on his behalf, "Sandy, well, he was Robert 'Bobby' Mayfield. George Mayfield's son. He changed his name years ago to Mitchell and moved away to Tassie. Where I guess he met you, Bette. I'm surprised you didn't suspect him yourself. He was hardly home, was he, always driving trucks interstate? But I guess he had to knock off his own father, in case he recognised Chris Burford, and maybe put two and two together. Might have asked the right questions. Sandy wanted the secret to remain well and truly buried with Munroe."

Bette shook her head and folded her arms. She was genuinely shocked by this new revelation and looked critically at Sandy, "You mean...you killed your own father, to keep a secret? You were prepared to kill me, as well? My God, this is complete madness."

"You're correct. Not just mad. He's a total psycho, and you were living with him. For years, you lived with...I guess you might call him a sleeping killer. That's what he is."

"Why did Sandy come back?" Raquel piped up.

Duncan continued, "It's no coincidence that he chose to return to Brumby Flat. He knew, sooner or later, Burford would try to return to town. He had been cut loose for a while and might reach out to his parents. He couldn't let that happen. His original intention was just to get rid of Chris but other people got in the way, unfortunately."

Bette was trying to stop her tears.

Proctor, gingerly holding his injured side, added with a wry smile, "Never mind, ma'am. At least you didn't have to play dead for real."

Proctor then winched, held Raquel tighter to him and spoke again, "Detective, I have to be honest with you too. I saw your Christopher drive into town. I saw Bette in the shop and Sandy was hiding across the road, just over there." He pointed to the other side of the main street with his good hand.

"Oh wow. You left that news a bit late to tell me. When were you planning to say something, to me?"

"Well, there's more…if you would care to hear about it. I have a bird's eye-view from those silos, you know. You get to see many interesting things from up there. And I believe you two know what I'm talking about."

Duncan blinked hard behind his glasses and looked as if he was about to drop his weapon. Raquel turned to look around at her friend Bette who suddenly looked rather pale.

Their big secret was out.

About twelve months later…

Raquel was driving back into Brumby Flat from her new IT job at the local winery. The passing landscape was a pleasing sea of green and neat fields of tall, willowy crops. Nearly twelve months had passed since that rainy night of drama in the Raindrops Shop. Her hair had grown past her shoulders and now she wore it in a loose ponytail. She had started to wear jeans again after twenty years.

She heard her mobile rang. The ringtone was Bette's favourite song.

"Hey, Bette, how are you going?" she answered brightly.

"Doll, yes, I'm very good. Now listen, I know that we haven't talked for a while…"

Raquel interrupted her, "Look, it's alright. I am sorry I made a fuss about it. You've got the right to go off and do whatever's right for you. I get that. But honestly, you shocked me when you said you were going on a date with Detective Phillip Duncan. I honestly didn't expect you to say that."

There was a silence on the other side of the line, which lasted a good ten seconds.

"Yeah, well, I quite understand your shock. I did not plan for anything like this to happen. You're my best friend in the world, you know. In fact, that's why I am calling you today."

Raquel knitted her eyebrows together, "You sound worried about something. Is everything okay?"

She heard Bette take in a deep breath, "It's wonderful news really, for me it is anyway. But I don't know if you'll be happy about it. Anyway, I'll be straight to the point. I am getting married next year. And I want you to be my Maid of Honour."

"Congratulations, thanks very much. I'd love to be there. My Phil hasn't asked me, but don't worry about it. I am so happy for you. So, who's the lucky guy? Is he the one you've been seeing in Adelaide recently?" she asked brightly.

There was another ten seconds worth of silence, before the surprising answer came, "Yes, he is. He's Senior Detective Phillip Duncan. He asked me, I like him. And he asked me. What do I say, doll?"

Raquel swallowed hard, "Well, you might have told him no. But I guess, you won't be doing that."

"Sandy's in jail. I've divorced him and I'm a free agent. That part of my life is over. Duncan has asked me to marry him and it surprises me, but we get on rather well together. I don't have any other options, doll. I am no spring chicken and I am lucky to get a second chance, with a man who says he loves me very, very much. I hope you can be just happy for me. You've got your man after all, haven't you?"

"Of course, congratulations to you both. Hope to catch up soon." Raquel replied tight-lipped.

They had both said goodbye and hung up as Raquel drove up Proctor's driveway. She hopped out of the car, not knowing how she should feel about this piece of news. She adored Phil Proctor but at that moment, she felt almost something like a sense of betrayal. It was not the kind of news she had expected from Bette. She decided not to give it any more thought.

She could tell that Proctor was back from the silos, seeing his pickup truck was parked neatly back in the garage. She heard the excited barking before she saw their dog Maxine trot into sight, wagging her tail furiously.

"Hey Max, you're a good girl," Raquel kneeled and stroked Maxine's sleek head, "Stay outside. We'll play later, hey?"

Maxine licked her hand as if she understood and wandered off, tail wagging.

She breezed in through the open front door and found Proctor standing in the kitchen, leaning casually back against the bench, cradling a mug of strong black tea. He had not changed physically or in his outlook since that fateful night in the Raindrops Shop when Sandy was caught and he was wounded. He had made a quick recovery and was back riding the black mare two months later and working on the silos project again.

She noticed he was wearing his favourite check western shirt, his Texas emblazoned buckle and leather belt looped through his latest pair of stonewashed Levi's. He had that pleasant horsey smell about him, so she knew he had gone for a quick ride. He looked up at her, with seriously brooding blue eyes. It was an unusual look coming from him.

"Hey," she said.

"Hey you," he smiled very slightly and put out his right forearm, to claim the curve of her waist. He pulled her in, bent his head over and gently kissed her forehead.

"How are you doing?" she asked him, hugging him.

"Great, my sweetheart. I should finish the town mural tomorrow. And I have some other news for you too."

Raquel peered up at him and found his facial expression too hard to read.

"What's up? I just had a bit of a shock from Bette. So Phil. What's your news then?"

Proctor pulled her closer against him, and her face nestled in his warm, heaving chest, "You know how much I care about you, my sweetheart."

"Of course," she closed her eyes, a tear welling in one corner and found it hard to swallow as she said the words, "I love you too."

Proctor went on, "But I have a difficult choice to make. I have been approached to do another silo project in the next district. That would mean, I would have work for another twelve months here. But I have to be truthful with you. I am missing New York. My real home. Been here for a while now. I still haven't seen that much of Australia and I sure as hell would like to. I need to know. If I decided to travel around this Aussie land a bit and go back home to New York, would you come back with me, girlie? Well? Would you entertain the idea?"

She backed out of his warm embrace and looked up at him, frowning. In the space of a few short minutes, she felt that her life had been completely turned upside down.

In a quiet, neutral tone, she said, "Phil, I need some time to take all this in."

...To be continued in the sequel, Pretty Dead Ordinary